Jessie had won.

She had won the game.

She had won Ewan's estate. His title. She wasn't even sure such a thing was possible. She was a woman.

And this was not the eighteen hundreds.

But it didn't matter.

And he was not... He was not disappointed.

She could see it.

Yes, he was affecting a laissez-faire sort of attitude. The posture of the kind of man who didn't care whether he won or lost anything.

But he didn't care. He had lost by design. And he had lost this very particular prize by design.

Against her will, she found herself intrigued by him.

From Destitute to Diamonds

Rags to riches and wearing his ring!

Sisters Jessie and Maren escaped their criminal father's clutches five years ago. Ever since, they've been on the run and using their genius minds to create their own futures. Now their livelihoods depend on two high-stakes poker games. These Cinderella sisters are expecting the games to completely change their lives...but perhaps not exactly in the way they do!

Don't miss these two captivating romances by Millie Adams:

The Billionaire's Accidental Legacy

When Jessie wins a Scottish estate, she claims a night with the previous playboy owner, Ewan. But their passion has a consequence that will bind them forever!

Available now!

The Christmas the Greek Claimed Her

Maren may have won a castle and become a princess, but there's one part of the fairy tale she hasn't written for herself: her unexpected marriage to Acastus Diakos!

Coming soon!

Millie Adams

THE BILLIONAIRE'S ACCIDENTAL LEGACY

HARLEQUIN
PRESENTS

Recycling programs
for this product may
not exist in your area.

ISBN-13: 978-1-335-59178-4

The Billionaire's Accidental Legacy

Copyright © 2023 by Millie Adams

For questions and comments about the quality of this book,
please contact us at CustomerService@Harlequin.com.

Harlequin Enterprises ULC
22 Adelaide St. West, 41st Floor
Toronto, Ontario M5H 4E3, Canada
www.Harlequin.com

Printed in U.S.A.

Millie Adams has always loved books. She considers herself a mix of Anne Shirley (loquacious but charming and willing to break a slate over a boy's head if need be) and Charlotte Doyle (a lady at heart but with the spirit to become a mutineer should the occasion arise). Millie lives in a small house on the edge of the woods, which she finds allows her to escape in the way she loves best— in the pages of a book. She loves intense alpha heroes and the women who dare to go toe-to-toe with them (or break a slate over their heads).

Books by Millie Adams

Harlequin Presents

His Secretly Pregnant Cinderella
The Billionaire's Baby Negotiation
A Vow to Set the Virgin Free

The Kings of California

The Scandal Behind the Italian's Wedding
Stealing the Promised Princess
Crowning His Innocent Assistant
The Only King to Claim Her

Visit the Author Profile page
at Harlequin.com for more titles.

CHAPTER ONE

JESSIE HARGREAVE HAD been taught to believe that there were two kinds of people. The *frightened* and the *frightening*.

Raised by a narcissistic, sociopathic millionaire crime lord, she and her sister Maren had been taught to hold the wants and needs of others in low esteem. All that mattered—all that could ever matter—was what *you* wanted. And what you could manipulate others into giving you.

Their soft, flighty mother had never been able to stand up to their father, and eventually she'd gone away. Off to greener pastures with easier rich men who didn't demand quite so much in return for a life of luxury.

That left Jessie and her sister behind.

"I am frightened now. And we aren't frightening," she could remember Maren whispering tearfully after she sneaked into Jessie's room the night their mother had left.

Poor Maren, who had the same peculiar mind as Jessie but with the focus skewed less toward facts and numbers and more toward human frailty and emotion. It overwhelmed poor Maren at times. Jessie felt like protecting her sweeter, softer sister was her greatest mission.

Eighteen months younger than she was, Maren was her baby sister, and Jessie would die for her if need be.

She just felt having minds like theirs meant no one should have to do anything half so dramatic as dying. They'd been given the gift of great thought. So they ought to be able to use it to solve their own problems.

"There must be a secret third option."

She'd said that so pragmatically she'd believed herself instantly.

"What is it, Jessie?"

"I don't know. I'll figure it out."

And so she had. They had.

They were neither frightened nor frightening. They had learned to thrive in the shadowy space between extremes.

They had become gray opportunists who used the frailties of those who fancied themselves as *frightening* against them.

Jessie hardly saw herself as Robin Hood, though she did *only* rob the rich. It was just she wasn't handing out alms to the poor. Unless she considered *herself* a member of the poor. And hey, for a long time, she had been.

But she wasn't now. Neither was her sister, thanks to all their work.

They'd spent the past three years playing in casinos and private high-stakes poker tournaments, amassing wealth, gambling it and turning it into yet more wealth.

This game was the last game.

She hadn't learned much from her father, other than what a person ought not to do.

She and Maren had decided at twelve and thirteen that they wouldn't be part of their father's games, but they'd also decided they'd have to have a clear path to escape before they tried to make a move.

Their father was like them. He didn't miss anything. They'd have one shot; it would have to be perfect. They'd had to get IDs—their father had never provided them with any—birth certificates, falsified naturally—and figure out where they would stay.

They squirreled their contraband beneath the floorboards of their bedroom in their father's compound, and then finally, they'd made a real plan of escape.

Their father used them to exploit banking systems—that was his world. He had an obscene amount of money and made more loaning it to people he could exploit for favors.

He used Maren and Jessie to help with those things.

Jessie could remember when her father had asked her to get all the info she could from talking to a certain man at a train station, and she had. She'd pretended to be lost and he'd talked to her to calm her down.

"His name is Marcus," she'd told her father. *"He has a granddaughter he loves very much. Her name is Eloise. She and her parents live in London."*

If only she'd known then how her father would use that information.

The images still haunted her. Every image did.

So she'd done what she always did. She used her brain to solve her problems.

She'd centered herself, and she'd gone into a big room in her mind and imagined a ribbon, made of pretty blue silk. She'd imagined it was tied to her feelings, connecting her thoughts to them. She'd taken out a pair of gleaming scissors and cut that ribbon. Severing it entirely.

She didn't need feelings anyway.

She and Maren had escaped five years ago, finally, at seventeen and eighteen. She had purpose. She didn't need feelings.

They would *not* be frightened.

They would *not* be poor. They would never be vulnerable or endangered, *ever*.

They would use every asset they had to make themselves safe and secure, to play their way to the kind of lives they really wanted.

They had also decided that there would have to be an endgame.

Because once you were willing to dip your toe into the murky waters of theft and con artistry, it was easy to lose yourself. Easy to drown. That was where crime lords came from. It was how your morals began to strip themselves away entirely.

She could not ever allow herself to be quite so lost.

So this was it. The last show.

Their long con had been shockingly easy. Because they were new, they were young and they were women. Beautiful women, at that.

It wasn't vanity for her to think so. Beauty was nothing but a well-fitted dress and some brightly colored makeup. In these circles, beauty could be put on and taken off like a costume, with relative ease.

No one was looking deeply at the features of her face. They were looking at her bold red lip and her cleavage. End of story.

The cleavage went a long way in ensuring she was underestimated. By all those men who were so sure they were smarter, better.

Men who believed that they could read any room. And above all else, men who believed they would always triumph.

She didn't feel guilty about it.

If you gambled, you might lose. And when you

underestimated an opponent on sight, you were a fool.

That was one saying she did believe to be true: a fool and his money were soon parted.

And if she was the instrument of that grand divorce, all the better.

Especially when it ended up in her pocket.

But they had decided there would be a limit.

This exclusive poker game had been an absolute mission to gain an invite to. Partly because she and her sister were not notorious.

That was important.

They had done their very best to move beneath the radar. They didn't want to draw the attention of their father, and in general Jessie found the concept of painting a target on your back foolish.

Young women getting big prizes at poker games might have been headline grabbing, were they not haunting private games, games played by royalty, by criminals. People who did not wish to have attention shown upon their habits.

They weren't masters of disguise; they didn't have to be.

A change in gown color, hair color and makeup meant that they were rarely remarked upon. They also hadn't played the same crowd twice.

Tonight would be different. Tonight would be high profile. And that was why tonight was the end.

But if they won, it would be by far their biggest score, and they would be able to be done with all of this.

To truly begin again.

Or rather, for the first time. A life that was theirs. Truly theirs.

It was Maren who had caught wind of tonight's game. A secret poker game being played at an old English estate house out in the countryside.

Invitation only.

Maren's special skill was her softness. She was lush and pretty and had wide, round eyes that always looked just a little bit wounded. Men loved a wounded bird. She would sigh and listen to them and express sympathy, and they would give her the world.

She'd been working at a gentlemen's club when she'd heard about the game.

She'd taken the job for information, of course. It could never be said that she or Maren had ever done an *honest* day's work in their lives.

Honest work didn't pay well enough.

Maren had the ability to get info out of anyone, using her soft voice and very large eyes. She was so good at seeming stupid. But then, was it their fault people often perceived the hallmarks of femininity as less? Maren used that, and she used it well.

She wasn't a siren; she was the sweet, childlike

one who needed to be shepherded along. And if she could be shepherded to lucrative poker tournaments…then all the better.

They weren't pickpockets. That was base.

And far too small.

With feigned interest, and a couple of well-placed giggles, Maren had found out about *this* game.

And about the invitation. And with her photographic memory, had committed the layout of the invitation to memory. As well as the particulars of how the invitations were disseminated and whether or not they would be able to make a counterfeit.

In the end, Jessie had taken the information and contacted the assistant of the organizer of the event, and managed to convince her to send out an invitation to her and her sister's aliases, on the pretense that their uncle had told them about the game. Of course, they had all of their fake uncle's details as well. Including the serial number on the ticket.

She smoothed her silver dress, and it shimmered over her curves like liquid metal.

Maren was in gold tonight, all the better to set off her red hair—fake, of course.

They were not there to look like sisters. Jessie had naturally dark brown hair, which for the night had been dyed black.

Maren's hair was a lighter shade of brown that skewed cinnamon nicely.

They would be playing in different halls tonight, at different tables. There was no point competing against each other.

Jessie knew just who she wanted to play today.

Ewan Kincaid. The Duke of Kilmorack.

A *duke*. It was so archaic and hilarious. He had spent the past few years whoring his riches out to any old table, disgracing his title and his father's name. He won vast sums, and was considered by many to be the best card player in high-stakes games. He was a wretched playboy. A debauched, dissolute gambler.

And absolutely the most beautiful man Jessie had ever seen.

She did her best not to think of him, but God help her, she did. Ever since she'd seen him for the first time in person.

She'd seen photos of him before, of course—he was infamous. Which was why that day on the casino floor fourteen months ago, she'd known instantly who he was.

But she hadn't been prepared for the impact of him.

Hadn't been able to forget.

He had been on the casino floor, not in a closed back room but in public for all to see. He liked a show. She did not. She'd been haunting the edges of that particular casino, hoping to sneak into a high-roller room, and there he was.

Head and shoulders above everyone around him, dressed in a close-cut black suit that showed off broad shoulders and a lean waist. He was devastating to her sanity. To her desire to be something other than what she had long feared she might be.

Wicked.

Across the room, their eyes collided. There was no other word for it. And in that moment a reel of fantasies she'd never had before played through her mind like a symphony. Building, building, exploding.

Images of his hands on her body. His broad shoulders without a suit jacket on…

He had consumed her from that moment.

She'd seen him again from afar in Monaco the next month. She'd made sure to keep her distance from him. She'd stared, from the upper floor in the casino down to where he was, until he turned and she'd run away.

Her breathing had been labored, her heart beating fast. Not from physical exertion.

From him.

And then there was Capri.

She'd been in a high-roller room at a table of whales, and she'd been winning. And he'd come and taken his position at another table. He'd seen her.

And later when she'd gone to collect her winnings, he'd followed her out.

"I know you."

It had been a singular moment. She'd been seen. And it was like that neatly trimmed blue ribbon had fashioned itself together in that moment, her heart taking flight along with her imagination.

Her breath had caught. *"You don't. I'm no one."*

"You were in Las Vegas. A few months back."

"I've never been to Vegas."

A lie. She'd been born in Reno. She'd been to Vegas more times than she could count. Even before all this.

And she'd been mesmerized by his eyes.

Blue. But on one side a fleck of green. On the other, gold.

"Liar."

"You have me confused with someone else."

"I am never confused."

He'd touched her then. The edge of his finger skimming her bare arm.

"I have to go. I have a prize to collect," she said.

"I wouldn't be opposed to adding myself to the prize packet."

Her heart had started pounding so hard she'd been dizzy.

"Not tonight."

And again, she'd run.

She'd acted like the *frightened*.

And she'd never wanted to be frightened.

It was one reason tonight she felt like she needed to conquer him. He'd scared her. He was under her skin.

She wanted him.

And she wanted to run from him.

Here she was, hoping to best him.

She had not, of course, said anything to her sister about his beauty.

Or her opinion on it.

They had rules about men.

Very strict rules. And she was…pushing things. She knew it.

She knew that she would have to start at an early round table, and that the likelihood of being placed with him immediately was low.

In fact, she wasn't entirely certain she would be put in his tier. But she had no problem putting herself there.

Her body went languid just thinking of being near him again.

She swept through the grand manor and took a glass of champagne off the tray. She was allowed three sips of champagne, and the rest of the night she simply mimicked the act of drinking.

One thing she had learned was that your behavior had to blend. Melt seamlessly in with the people around you. They were narcissists. Every last one of them. All humans were. To one extent or another. And they were always much more concerned with their own behavior than with yours. But it was important that they didn't feel you challenge their behavior. To make declarations about not drinking made others uncomfortable. Who were constantly then attempting to justify their actions and paint them as being inside normality.

And so Jessie pretended to drink. In fact, she found it was a boon because the more she drank, the more those around her often felt comfortable drinking. And she was always happy to have her opponents' wits slightly addled.

Not that she needed it.

She could win even if everyone was playing their best. But what she didn't want them to note was why she won. And how she did so with ease.

She always lost a couple of times. Enough to throw off suspicion.

She sidled up to the waiter. Not one of the waitresses, and not one of the straight men. She knew exactly who to speak to. She needed someone who wouldn't feel threatened by her beauty, but also wouldn't want it for himself.

"I know that we are not supposed to do this, but do you know which table Ewan Kincaid is playing at?"

The man looked at her, and his eyebrows lifted.

"If you know you're not supposed to do it, why are you doing it?"

"I'm sorry." She tried to look both ditzy and overcome. "I have a bit of a crush on him. And I just want to make sure that I can sit at his table for a moment. I'm not very good. Honestly, I'm only here to...you know."

His smile went naughty. "You want to get lucky."

"I do," she said, smiling.

Definitely not in the way he meant. But yes. She was here to get lucky.

"He's been placed in the West Wing game. It's really high stakes. But he is..."

"So hot, right? I'm not worried. I can buy my way into any of these rooms. I was invited, after all."

"And you're just here to throw it away on a night in his bed?"

"I hear he's worth it."

"He definitely looks like he is, but you know he gives it away for free."

"No one gives anything *good* away for free."

"I suppose that's true."

She put her hand on his forearm. "Thanks. So much."

She wiggled away from him, unable to take large steps in the very tight dress.

Hopefully, he wouldn't get in any trouble. But the exchange had been brief enough. She had not been placed in the West Wing. But she managed to talk her way past the door, and get a seat set up, all by giggling and claiming it was because of her little crush.

Her fingers tingled. She felt alive right now. She was so good at this.

She was…

She was done.

After this she was done. They'd agreed.

If she won tonight, she'd won the whole game. She had to remember that.

At the end of this she would have a whole new life. So much money. And she would never gamble any of it again.

This was the game they'd been planning for two years now. Win, invest. Win, invest. In clothes, and access to the right rooms. In the ability to have enough money to buy their way into the games in the first place.

But this was the thing with gambling. So Maren reminded her. Eventually, you had to call it good. Had to call it a day. And you had to walk away.

Especially when you gambled the way they did.

Her father was brilliant. He could've used his brain for anything. But the problem was, he was more than a narcissist. He was a sociopath, and he enjoyed testing people. He needed to do it. He was smarter than everyone else and he was desperate to prove it.

They weren't the same.

She was nearly certain.

Sure, she got satisfaction out of winning, but she didn't need to do it. She wanted to be happy. She wanted to be comfortable.

She wanted to be *free*.

And if she felt a tug of sadness over losing this…

The thrill of a mark. The thrill of the chase…

Well, she wouldn't dwell on it.

This wasn't a charity game, and no one here was playing for any reason other than that they could. They treated their wealth lightly, and they treated the lives of others as if they were nothing.

Ewan Kincaid was a fantastic example of that. His family name was old, respected, and he dragged it through the mud.

His industry was debauchery.

Bars and party yachts and exclusive clubs where the very rich could act out their wildest fantasies.

Everything about him was a scourge on respectability.

If she had come from a family like his, she would've treated it with some care. He respected nothing, including his fortune. Which he now slung hither and yon with as much care as his penis.

None whatsoever.

He was not discerning.

She reminded herself of that when his face presented itself clearly in her mind's eye. He was a rake.

It shouldn't excite her.

Just like gambling shouldn't excite her.

But both did.

She sat down at her assigned table, and smiled at the men around her.

Ewan was not among them; he must be at one of the other tables in the room, but that didn't matter. It was perfect. She was opening at a table of all gray-haired men who would assume she was even younger than she was, and likely twice as dumb.

She played it up, giggling and making her movements seem nearly childish.

Men loved that.

A woman who acted like a girl but had big boobs. She and Maren had gotten their minds from their father. And their figures from their mother. And she supposed in the absence of any moral character, she should be thankful for those two gifts they had received from their parents.

Because those assets certainly made cons easier.

She lost the first hand deliberately. And then won all over the next two games, advancing to the next table.

Where she cut a swath through the tournament like a shark.

There was so much money. So very much money.

And finally, the room was down to one table. And when she sat down, she felt as if the entire world had been tilted on its axis.

Because there he was.

And no amount of press coverage, of illicitly taken viral videos of him caressing women on dance floors of his clubs, or photographs of him in the media could prepare for the impact of him in person.

Her memory was perfect.

And even her memory hadn't captured this.

The man was an absolute thirst trap. Which was public knowledge.

But that was all looks. A still photo could never capture this.

The magnetism.

His dark brown hair was pushed off his forehead, and she could see strands of gray, just there at his temples, adding an air of sophistication to the man sitting before her. His blue eyes held anything but sophistication. They were wicked. And filled with promises that made her feel overheated.

The lines around his eyes spoke of secret smiles shared with countless lovers. And she trembled. He didn't move, and she tried, tried her very best, to remain still, and yet could not. She had a will of iron. She always had. Her brain was always a flurry of activity. It was like that when you could remember everything. Unavoidable.

And yet, because of her memory, it was very difficult to surprise her. She'd seen him before, after all.

Her observational skills were unparalleled. And the speed at which she synthesized all the images in her brain made it so she was always one step ahead.

But right now she was breathless. Right now there was no thought beyond him.

And she could not recall a time when she held just one single thought, not ever, not once in her whole life.

"Hello there," he said, that rough Scottish accent making her feel as warm as it had the first time she'd heard it.

He knew her.

She could see that.

She pretended.

"Hello," she said, allowing herself to blush. It was the easiest thing.

The easiest thing ever, as she searched his face. She'd memorized every detail the first time she'd seen him. It was what she did.

Every line, every minute piece of him.

And yet, now she did it again. As if she was committing him to memory for the first time.

The green fleck in his left eye, the gold in his right.

The slight impression of a scar on the right side of his upper lip. Not a razor blade. Nothing surgical. A fight. She knew exactly what a scar that came from a fist hitting flesh looked like.

She knew what her memory, what her words, could bring about.

She knew what it sounded like when a girl was being tortured for the sins of her grandfather.

You saved her.

At least there's that.

But she'd been caused pain, and that couldn't be erased.

Her eyes dropped down to his hands, the way he touched the deck of cards.

Ewan touched her once…

No, that wasn't what she should be thinking of.

He wasn't the dealer. You did not deal your own cards in a game this high stakes. And yet, he was touching the deck of cards and no one had tried to stop him.

"Can I get your name?" He was looking at her as if she was the only other person at the table. There were others.

With her peripheral vision she had taken in every detail of their appearance. They did not signify. They did not register.

It was him and only him.

And she saw something just then. A light in

those eyes. A brighter glint to the cold. Something sharper in the green.

He moved around like he was a feckless playboy, like he chanced into his winnings, but he didn't.

She could see it.

He was a predator, this man.

And he made her shiver.

She watched his hands closely, seeing if anything came out of his sleeves. If there were any extra cards.

"Cat got your tongue, my beauty?"

"No," she said, forcing herself to meet his gaze. "I confess I'm a bit overwrought. You are quite famous."

Her words were breathy, and incredibly false, and she had to wonder if he could sense that.

Maybe he didn't recognize her.

Her hair had been red when they'd last met.

"Overwrought?" His mouth quirked upward. "You don't seem the type."

"Surely that's something you're used to. Women losing their powers of speech when in your presence."

"Yes. But there isn't usually a card table between us then. In fact, there's usually nothing between us by the time their speech fails them."

She couldn't control her response to him. And she controlled everything.

She was not inexperienced with men by accident.

On the contrary, she knew everything there was to know about men in an academic sense.

But she and her sister had rules. An agreement.

The problem with a mind like theirs was that they did hang on to every detail.

Trauma, they had decided, would be a particular beast when one couldn't forget. They'd already had their share.

They were far too clear on everything that had ever happened in their childhoods. They did not need to go tempting memories of an infatuation. Of heartbreak.

Sexual encounters that would burn each minute detail into their brains.

That would always live there. In that vast catalog of drawers in the back of her head.

Her sister had a *mind palace*.

Jessie thought it was a stupid name. And she thought it was a waste of imagination. Her sister kept all of her memories in a great library in a castle out in the middle of the sea. It was all bright and airy and *pink*.

Maren was a romantic. Maren was *good*.

Jessie was more pragmatic. Sometimes she worried if her sister was good, she might be wicked. So she leaned into the organizational aspects of her personality rather than the wickedness. She liked a file cabinet. And alphabetizing.

Not a color-coded organization system that made absolutely no sense.

He was red, she decided just then, and she was annoyed.

She didn't want to assign a color to him.

Red was intrusive. Strong. It was passion. Anger.

And she knew right then he would be filed under red forever, and she was deeply, deeply irritated about it.

Maren would think it was hilarious.

This was why they had rules about men.

An agreement. Until they had succeeded in getting themselves secure, they stayed well away from them.

The risk was too high. For them especially.

They could not afford to be compromised before they had finished.

Before they were safe. Before they were secure.

"I have to confess," she said, hoping that this would throw him off. And make him complacent about her skills. "I might have worked my way into this room just to sit with you. I'm a fan."

"Well, then, I'll be sure to sign something for you later."

His eyes caught hers, and held.

Everything in her went still.

Her throat dry and scratchy.

"Aren't you going to take the cards from him?" she asked the dealer.

She'd betrayed more of herself then than she would have liked.

"Of course," said the dealer, removing the cards from the center of the table. Was everyone under his spell? No one seemed concerned.

He lifted a brow in question. And she tried to simper.

"Just wanted to make sure you don't have anything up your sleeve," she said, trying to keep her tone sweet.

"I never have anything secreted away except for an extra bottle of whiskey. You have no need to worry."

No. She decided then that he wouldn't cheat. Not like that. It would be clumsy and inelegant.

But there were other ways. And she knew them all.

Gameplay began. The cards were dealt. And bidding began.

He was relaxed. And he didn't have a tell. But she was keeping track of where the cards were.

And everyone else had easy tells.

By process of elimination, she had figured out several hands.

When the dealer dealt the cards, all she had to do was keep watch on the edges.

It was easy for her to approximate where they then folded and who they went to. What was still in the deck and what might still be at hand.

It required concentration, but if she lost it at

any point, she could simply call back the image in her mind.

Right now Ewan had a particularly good hand.

There were a couple of cards she could not account for, of course, but she had a fair idea of everything that was happening.

And so, when the bidding became intense, she folded.

She would have one more round to take all.

And this was where things became complicated.

Knowing when to trade. When to hold. When to fold.

He won, quickly and decisively. And he took the pot to himself.

Good. Let him think it would go his way.

Her adrenaline spiked.

Several left the table. Done for the evening.

Two were eliminated.

And there she remained. Her heart beating faster, her blood singing. She was doing it. Like she always did. It felt so good.

Winning.

The next hand went out.

She nearly breathed a sigh of relief. She almost had a full house. One card short. And if she traded… It was still there. It was in the deck.

"I'll take one," she said.

She slid the card forward.

And the one that came back to her was exactly what she had hoped for.

She kept her face impassive, and then allowed her forehead to pucker. Let him wonder.

Bidding began in earnest with many more people making trades.

Another round, three folded.

The pot was growing, bigger and bigger.

She was getting to the top of her budget.

And suddenly, it was just her and him. Seated across from each other with chips in between them. Her whole future riding on this moment and yet…

Right now the moment felt bigger than her future. It was just her and him. This man she'd set out to conquer. This man who haunted her.

You'll either lose everything or you're finished.

She was finished either way. She'd vowed to be finished.

She didn't have any more money to gamble with. Any more and she would be reaching into Maren's pot, and she had no way of knowing how steep of a game her sister was involved in.

They were the only two left.

She prayed he would call.

"I raise you," he said.

The amount of money he raised exceeded what she had. By so much it was impossible.

She could win this. She wouldn't fold.

She wouldn't lose.

And that meant… That meant it was time to take a risk.

"I… I see you," she said, her eyes locking with his. "And I raise you…my body."

CHAPTER TWO

IT WAS HER. He knew the moment he saw her. The woman from the casinos, all those months ago. Months in between, and he had not forgotten her. He couldn't. She'd changed her appearance. Her makeup, her hair, the style of dress. She'd altered her appearance all three times he'd seen her and still he'd known.

You could not cover the electricity that arced between them with a change of hair color. He'd seen her that first time on the casino floor and it had been like a match strike against the hardest part of him.

But it was more than sex.

He could have sex anytime he wanted. But this… This was something more.

She intrigued him.

And it took a lot to intrigue him.

She was a bold thing. And there was something else to her, and had been from the moment they'd met.

She saw him.

Ewan had been an emotional child. He'd been filled with sadness, laughter, anger and above all else, hope.

His mother had died and he'd wept until he couldn't breathe, and then his father had beaten him until his tears had mixed with blood.

He'd stopped showing how much he cared that day.

And he'd begun plotting revenge.

The facade of the playboy was a perfect one. People underestimated him. It was how he'd made his own private fortune in investments. In the beginning people were always willing to sell to him for a bargain-basement price and think they were fleecing him.

Ewan had come out on top, every time.

He laughed easily, he smiled, he made merry with every woman he encountered, but it was a surface kind of pleasure.

When he'd touched *her*, it had gone down to his bones.

She had ignited an intensity in him he'd thought long banished.

For her part, she'd seemed nervous, and he could see that she had also tried to make him feel certain she was ditzy.

She'd had different energy the other times he'd seen her, and he knew she was nothing that she appeared to be on the surface.

The woman was like a lure, twisting beneath

the surface of a loch. Sun catching her sparkles and making her shine.

There was a hook buried in there, though, he knew.

She was not dithery and she wasn't inexperienced at cards. She was brilliant. Sharp. She had taken every man at the tables to get here, and she would take him, too.

He would ensure it.

Ewan Kincaid was an expert at reading people. And all of their desires.

He was certain of two things when it came to this woman.

She was a liar. And she wanted him.

She had from the very first.

And she was not at all what she seemed to be.

"You are offering…?"

"One night. My body. Whatever you wish." She looked at him from beneath her lashes and he could see glitter there. Not just attraction. Something else.

She knew she was going to win so her offer wasn't sincere.

And yet, it was.

She would have him, if they were alone. She wanted him, desperately, and that was the only honest thing on her face.

"Unorthodox. Imagine if Sir William was still in the game."

"He is not," she said. "You are. It is a specific bet. For you to win…or lose."

She said it with no clear hint of provocation and that, in and of itself, was a red flag to a bull. She was so cool. A mystery. An intrigue.

All so hard to come by for his jaded palate.

"I see. So you have no more money."

"I confess, I find myself unable to raise you." She didn't sound worried. She seemed cool. Collected. At ease.

She wasn't afraid to lose, which meant she knew she wouldn't.

Or she wanted him that badly. But with the amount of money at stake, he doubted it.

He did not have a reputation for coming at a high cost.

"You may have to forfeit the game, then. Because I could simply offer more money. But then, that would require I determine the set value of your body."

"This is unorthodox," said the dealer.

Men like him were not paid to deal in the unorthodox. Thank God Ewan's life was more interesting than that.

"You do not have to facilitate," Ewan said, looking at the man. "The lady and I will work out our own terms."

Everyone around the table was staring at them, hushed.

Watching this woman prostitute herself.

But then, she had said that she'd attempted to get to his table. Was it for this purpose? Was this all an attempt to seduce him? Because this was quite a lot more work than most women put in to get into his bed.

He was notoriously easy.

He was a man who liked to party. A man who liked the pleasures of the flesh in all ways.

He liked women. He liked sex.

In vanilla and every other flavor that might be on offer.

All she would've had to do was walk in and ask for sex; he'd have given it to her.

He was hungry. Always. For every experience that might be out there. So it could only be that.

Plus, she was far too good at playing cards.

Far too good.

She was a card counter. That made sense.

The way that she looked at him, and everything else, was sharp and astute. He'd have likely lost to her even if he had *not* intended to lose tonight. His next offer had always been one he'd intended to make. Losing the estate was his goal, and doing so in a way that would make headlines.

It was a shame he had no intention of taking victory here. Because he wouldn't mind winning her body.

"You're right. It is impossible to volley with something of equal monetary value. And so my return offer is this. Upon my father's death, my title and my estate."

Her response to that was imperceptible. As he knew it had to be.

If she appeared surprised, or too eager, then it would be easy for the casual observer to see that she was certain she had a win on her hands. She was very good, this woman.

If she lost, she would be his for the night.

But he did not think she would.

He had, by design, lost a good deal of money over the past few months. It mattered little to him. Money was easily had. The entire point was to make it look as if he was on the verge of a break-down. That he was careening right off the edge of a cliff, and that he would take his dying father's title and empire with him. The old man only had a couple of weeks left. Long enough to see him lose the estate. Long enough to know that it would be leaving the family. They had an archaic inherited title that meant nothing.

But he had already vowed to his old man that he would never have a child, never pass the estate on. The bloodline would end with him.

Of that he would make sure.

"I call," she said.

"Then put your cards on the table."

And when she did, a gasp went through the room.

She had done it.

She was dizzy. She could hardly breathe. She had won and the triumph of it was intoxicating beyond reason.

She had won.

She had won the game.

She had won his estate. His title. She wasn't even sure such a thing was possible. She was a woman.

And this was not the eighteen hundreds.

But it didn't matter.

And he was not… He was not disappointed.

She could see it.

Yes, he was affecting a laissez-faire sort of attitude. The posture of the kind of man who didn't care whether he won or lost anything.

But he didn't care. He had lost by design. And he had lost this very particular prize by design.

Against her will, she found herself intrigued by him.

Even as she was trying to grapple with the fact that she had just won millions of dollars. And an estate.

She had a home.

After all these years, Jessie Hargreave had a home.

And they really could be finished. Even if Maren didn't win her game.

"Congratulations, Miss…"

"Lockwood," she said. "Jessica Lockwood."

She found it best to keep the first name as close as possible to her actual name.

Anyway, the world was littered with Jessicas.

But her last name was one of her many aliases.

"Thank you," she said to the dealer.

"Your winnings will be wired to the bank account information that you provided earlier. As to the rest of the…unconventional bet. That will be up to you and the duke."

He grinned at her, slow and lazy.

She needed to find her sister.

"Have the other games concluded?"

The man checked his watch. "No. There is a particularly fierce game going on in the East Wing. It does not look as if it will conclude anytime soon."

"Thank you."

She didn't necessarily wish to go and connect herself to Maren. So they would have to convene when they could.

And she was grateful in some ways that this moment was hers and hers alone.

She loved her sister. Her sister was never tempted to bask in these sorts of moments. She was never tempted to glory in the wrong things. Jessie couldn't say the same for herself.

And when she looked at Ewan Kincaid, she felt like indulging in the wicked even more than usual.

Her heart was thundering hard. She had bet

herself. Her body. She had known she wouldn't lose. With almost complete certainty.

There was that possibility. That small possibility. That she might've lost. And she would've honored the bet.

The very idea sent a jolt of something sensual through her.

She had never been touched intimately by a man before.

Had never kissed one.

She wanted to.

She and Maren had worked so hard, all this time, and Maren had been very clear they needed to draw lines, and Jessie agreed. She did.

But she was tempted. And this was the last night, the last hurrah. The last window.

She should be overjoyed to walk away, and while on some level she was, while she was buzzing with the absolute triumph of all that she had just achieved, she felt sorrow as well. For this was where she shone.

It was where she was the best. She wasn't afraid here. She wasn't small. Not the insignificant unwanted daughter of a crime lord who had wanted a son, but had seen value in herself and her sister because of their minds.

No, she was using her mind on her own terms, and using it to benefit her.

It made her feel good. She could admit that now, without her sister close by her.

It thrilled her. Hell, a win like this turned her on.

And sitting across from the man who had ignited her imagination from the moment she had first seen him…

This was it. She would never run into him again. She would have no reason to. But tonight she would have reason to convene with him privately regarding her win. They would be alone…

"Shall we adjourn?" she said.

"Anxious?" he asked.

His manner was smooth. Unruffled. He didn't seem to care that he had just lost…everything.

"Yes. I would hate for you to back out. You seem awfully resigned for a man who has just lost his title and his estate."

The corner of his mouth lifted upward. "You assume that I care about those things."

"I suppose when you have so much it's easy to disavow the care of something others would find essential."

He ignored that.

"I have a suite of rooms upstairs. You will join me there. Perhaps for a drink as well as a discussion."

"Yes. I would like that."

He stood, and her mouth went dry. She had forgotten how tall he was. How broad.

He was nothing like the other men here. Who were either overstuffed with their imports and rich foods or self-consciously lean in a testament to their dedication at finding some sort of meaning of life in fitness. Accomplished from cycling in too-fitted Lycra and days spent playing pickleball.

But not so, Ewan Kincaid.

Who looked as if he spent his days out in fields lifting boulders. Moving them about the Highlands.

The Highlands.

Scotland.

That would be where his home was. His ancestral dwelling.

She had never been to Scotland.

It was, she thought, such a fascinating thing to have inherited. And it was the kind of decisive victory she could not have ever dreamed of. Not only had she more money than she'd ever seen in her life, but she also had a home.

He moved to her, putting his hand on her lower back, and everything in her went molten.

It was as if someone had reached inside her and taken everything she knew and squeezed it down tightly in their hand, so that it became small.

And she became reckless.

She would never be here again. Never have this moment again. Where she was the winner. She had claimed victory over him. And why could he not be her prize as well?

She had been prepared to surrender her body

to him on the very off chance that she had lost the match.

In fact, part of her had been excited by it.

It was that sort of wickedness that she had always been afraid lurked in her veins.

And it did. In this moment it did. It was burning to the surface. Why not indulge it?

Because this was why they had decided they had to end the charades. It became too much a part of who you were.

If this was her last moment to be wicked, then why not dive in? Put her head under water. Drown in it.

They wove their way through the crowd, and into an elevator.

Everyone had been looking at them, but pretending they were not.

"What is your real name?" he asked, when the doors closed on them.

"I told you my name."

"It is not your name. I've seen you before." The breath left her body. "This is what you do. And your name is not Jessica Lockwood."

"Does it matter what my name is?"

"You want legal ownership of the estate? This is not money wired into your fake account. You want your name on the deed."

She froze. "I cannot have my name easily found. I'm certain you will understand."

"I'm happy to wrap it up in a business of some

kind. But your legal name ought to be buried somewhere in there, don't you think?"

"I'm nobody. Nobody to you. But I am somebody who might be harmed if I'm found by the wrong person."

"A con artist."

"Nothing about what I did was a con. I beat you."

"But how?"

She lifted her chin. "By having better cards than you."

"Yes, that would be the assumed way. But you also won the game at the casino in Vegas. In Capri. And then again in Monte Carlo."

"You saw me."

"I always see you." It was like the world stopped, right then. And she would be just fine if it never started again. His voice lowered, his eyes meeting hers. "Redhead, brunette." He reached out and touched her hair. "Raven's wing. It doesn't matter. You are not an easy woman to forget."

She was a woman who couldn't forget. She had often wondered what it would be like to have the sort of brain that protected you from trauma. From pain. That shielded you from what you'd seen or heard.

She would never know.

She had a clear accounting of all of it, filed

away forever. A constant cluttering of details in her mind, no matter what.

But she would be happy to remember this.

To remember him telling her that she was hard to forget.

"If I give you my name, you must swear you will not let it get out. You must protect me."

"Darling, this will be in the news."

She knew that what he said was true, and that there was no way around it.

"And that's fine. My father… My father will not pay attention to a news story about the duke losing his family home, but if my name appears…"

"Jessica Lockwood will be your name as far as the public is concerned. But I want to know your real name."

Just then the doors opened. They walked out into an empty hall, and he paused in front of the door, pressing a key card to it, and she heard the lock give.

They walked into a modern-looking penthouse, so different than the rest of the estate home.

But clearly, the upstairs had been remodeled as a place for guests to stay.

"You have my word," he said, turning to face her. "I have no wish to harm you."

"Why would I believe that? Why would I believe it given that you just lost a game today, and you accused me of being a con artist?"

He treated her to another wicked grin. "Because one con artist recognizes another."

She scoffed. "You're not that good."

"I'm only not that good if I intended to win. Tonight… Tonight I intended to lose. My entire life is a con, lass. Make no mistake."

The way he said that, the way his Scottish accent rolled over the syllables, sent a shiver through her body.

This was all so dangerous, and the danger of it made her heart beat faster, but not with fear.

She wanted to remember tonight.

She wanted this last night to be bold and bright forever.

"Keep me safe," she whispered, "and you can have what you failed to win."

He lifted a brow, and then walked over to a bar in the corner. He picked up a decanter of whiskey, poured a measure of it and took a drink. "Are you offering me your body?"

She lifted her chin. "Yes."

"What sort of man do you take me for that you think you might need to trade sex for safety?"

"A man."

He took a step toward her, his eyes never leaving hers even as he took another drink of whiskey. "No. Darling, you're welcome to give me your body because you wish to give it. Because you cannot say no to the desire that has taken you over. But you will not trade me for your safety.

I am the most debauched man on the continent. I can have whoever I wish. Whenever I wish. I do not need a body offered to me as a sacrifice. I give you your safety. Freely. I do not want my estate. I lost it, and in the most scandalous way possible in order to destroy my father."

"I won," she said, aware that she sounded like a petulant child. Unable to do anything else.

"You did."

"You couldn't have beat me if you tried."

"I have no trouble believing that. I chose to stay in the game when I knew that I would lose. But losing was the only thing on my cards tonight."

She was shocked to discover the revelation didn't diminish the thrill of her victory. She had beaten everyone in there tonight to get over to his table. He had his own game. But then, so did everyone.

It was the way of it.

If anything, this made it all the more exciting.

"Before anything," he said. "Your name."

She trembled. On a knife's edge. Did she tell him? Or did she not?

The trouble was, she trusted him.

Even if she didn't know why.

"Jessie," she said. "Jessie Hargreave. *Jessica*, actually. So you had half the truth as it was."

"You're smart. Don't deviate too far from the truth if you wish to create a convincing lie."

"A very basic truth."

"Your father wishes to hurt you?" he asked.

"He's a dangerous man. Though I would say it's more he doesn't like to lose. And he lost me. He will want me back, I'm afraid."

"He would be Mark Hargreave, I assume."

She should have been prepared for that, and yet she wasn't. "Yes. I'm not surprised that you've heard of him. And you can understand why I don't let my name lead."

"I do. And now you have my word, he will not find you. You will be protected."

"Thank you."

"Here's the paperwork."

He turned to a locked cabinet, produced a key from his pocket and proceeded to release it.

He opened the doors and brought a stack of papers out before her. "You will sign it. With your legal name. And you will be assured that it is yours."

"All to get back at your father?"

He chuckled, and the sound made her body liquid. "I don't think I'm the only one here with daddy issues."

The word shimmered through her body.

The way that he looked at her, those enticing, unforgettable eyes looking into her.

She let out a breath and took hold of the papers, looking them over.

"Can you really give your title to me?"

"I've no idea. But you can claim it."

"And what is the purpose of this?"

"Revenge. Quite simply. My father is on his deathbed. This paperwork, by the way, ensures that it all passes to you upon his death. An agreement between yourself and me. We will have final papers sent to you once he draws his last breath. But I will ensure that he is aware that the line is ending with me, before he slips into hell. That's all I ask."

"That seems fair to me." She didn't need to question why the man hated his father. People were entitled to hate their fathers. God knew she hated her own.

She looked over the paperwork quickly, and signed.

The air between them became thick.

"I'm leaving gambling behind me," she said, stepping away from him, arousal making her warm.

This had been the most exciting night of her life. And he was an unexpected and thrilling opponent.

They had both won a victory tonight. And why should they not bask in it?

"Are you?"

She shrugged. "You have to stop eventually."

"Do you? I don't intend to stop until I drive my Ferrari into a brick wall. And then maybe I'll slow down."

"When you're dead?"

He shrugged. "Perhaps."

"That doesn't seem a recipe for a happy life."

"I don't want a happy life. I want *everything*. When I want it. All the time. I want excess. However long that lasts, I don't care. But a man like me isn't exactly made to sit in a rocking chair in his twilight years. A man like me isn't made for twilight years."

"That seems grim."

"Perhaps I'm grim. Maybe that's my secret. But in between the moments of grimness, I'm told I can be a good time."

"Show me." Her pulse was pounding.

"Why don't you show me?"

With his whiskey firmly in hand, he turned away from her, went and sat on a large armchair in front of windows that overlooked the back courtyard.

"I am told," he said, "these windows overlook the valley below. And we are on a cliff's edge. So no one can see. That's what I'm told. I suppose we can't be certain."

He took a sip of whiskey, those eyes burning into her. "Show me the prize I failed to win."

He was asking her to strip.

She didn't know how to strip. She had played the coquette, she had played the seductress, but none of the games that she and her sister played ever demanded that they follow through.

Tonight wasn't a game. Tonight was a claiming. She was cashing out. Why not cash out her virginity as well?

She reached behind her back, and before she could allow nerves to overtake her, she began to unzip the dress. She let it go loose, let it fall to her waist, her breasts bared for his perusal.

"Gorgeous," he said, his jaw going tense.

She knew the rumors about him, and he did as much as confirm them just now.

He was a man who did what he wanted, when he wanted to do it. He'd had more sex than he could likely catalog in an evening's time.

And he was aroused by the sight of her naked body.

He shifted, and she could see the evidence of his arousal, just there at the apex of his thighs.

She trembled.

"More," he demanded.

She pushed the gown down over her hips, so that she was wearing nothing more than the small white thong she put on earlier, and her sky-high heels.

She hadn't intended for anyone to see this. It made her feel sexy. Helped her play the part.

But now it felt as if it was for him. As if perhaps it always had been.

He lifted his hand, and crooked his finger. "Come here."

Jessie was not, as a general rule, obedient. But his voice was liquid velvet, and it poured over her like a soft, sensual promise, and she could not deny him.

She took a step toward him, and then another.

Until she was standing just before him, wearing nothing but those very brief underwear.

"It's a good thing I didn't intend to win, Ms. Hargreave. Because I would've found it nearly impossible to concentrate with you sitting across from me. And seeing you uncovered… You're even more exquisite than I could've imagined."

"Why do you remember me?"

She remembered everything. Everybody.

But she remembered him different. She remembered him red.

He didn't go in a file cabinet. He never could. He couldn't be classified, alphabetized, organized.

He was heat and light and burning passion, whether she wanted him to be or not.

And she knew that not everybody remembered the way that she did. But he remembered her. Surely it meant something.

She needed it to mean something.

"Because I want you," he said.

"You want me?"

"From the first moment I saw you. At that casino in Las Vegas. I was in the high-roller room, and I had won a ridiculous sum of money in the sort of game that makes my father livid.

"And I saw you there. You looked so young.

So innocent. But you aren't. You are an enigma. And you have been to me from that first moment.

"You wore a wig then. You don't wear one now."

She shook her head. "It's dyed darker now."

"Your hair looked short. Just to your chin then."

She nodded. "That was a wig."

"It was very pretty. Though I prefer this."

She shook her head, made her inky dark hair shimmer over her breasts like an oil spill. He growled, his hips bucking upward.

She had never felt so beautiful. And more to the point, she had never cared whether or not she felt beautiful. It had been a tool. Always. This body. This face.

It had never been anything she cared about.

"And then when I saw you again. In Monte Carlo. You were up on the second floor."

"When did you see me? I didn't…"

She hadn't realized.

She'd made mistakes with him. She had never made mistakes with anyone else before.

And she was standing naked before him now, and that should serve as a warning. A warning that he wasn't safe. That she needed to guard herself. She didn't make mistakes, and yet she did with him.

She didn't make mistakes, and yet she was standing before him naked.

Almost naked.

Her pulse was throbbing between her legs, and she wanted nothing more than to move forward and straddle his lap. Rub herself against him and satisfy the ache within her.

She was familiar with the desires of her body.

In her imagination it was vivid.

But this… This transcended imagination.

It was big and bright and real. It was red.

Suddenly, he reached out, his large hands gripping her hips and pulling her forward. And then he pressed his mouth to her stomach. Just beneath her belly button.

She shivered.

He had yet to kiss her lips, and yet his mouth, hot and impertinent, had touched her stomach.

"You are delicious," he said roughly. He looked up at her, moved his hands up her waist, just beneath the swells of her breasts. Her nipples went tight.

"Get down on your knees."

"I…"

"You have to earn it. Your right to be here. With me. Show me how much you want me. Show me you could be a good girl."

Her knees were trembling as she sank down before him, and he looked down at her, then reached out to cup her chin. Tilted her face upward. And closed the distance between them as he bent down to press his mouth to hers.

It was firm. Hot. And then he angled his head, and it became fury.

He parted her mouth roughly, pushing his tongue deep. A raw cry escaped her throat, and she kissed him back. Allowing him access. Surrendering to him.

She had thought to seduce him tonight, but this was different. She had thought to claim a prize, but he was nothing of the kind.

He was living and breathing and powerful. The furthest thing from cold, soulless money as one could be.

And he was not biddable. Pliable. She could not manipulate him.

That thrilled her deeper than anything else ever could have.

It had been exciting, knowing she had beaten him.

It was intoxicating to know she couldn't.

That he was a man with his own game running. A man with his own set of rules.

That he was perhaps her equal.

You're kneeling before him.

Yes. But because she chose to.

He began to undo the buckle on his pants, as he took his mouth away from hers.

He undid the button, the zipper, and revealed his hard, thick length.

She knew exactly what he wanted. And she wanted to give it to him.

She was about to lean forward, when he reached behind her head and pushed his fingers deep into her hair, drawing her head toward him, bringing her mouth down to him.

She parted her lips, and took the head of him in, that salty, musky flavor sending a sharp burst of desire through her. "Go ahead, pretty girl. Give me what I want."

With trembling hands, she wrapped her fingers around his thick shaft and began to work him as she sucked him into her mouth. She knew what a blow job was. She knew how they worked. She didn't have to have had personal experience giving one to know that.

She took him in as deep as she possibly could, and then… Then she lost herself.

It was like the light in that back room of her brain had been turned off. She couldn't see the file cabinets. She couldn't access the vast bank of memories that drove her, that assaulted her at all times. There was nothing but this. The taste of him. The feel of him. She had never done this before, and it was wholly new. Wholly terrifying. Wholly wonderful.

She was lost in the taste of him. The hardness. The heat.

The deep growl that he made in the back of his throat when she did something he liked.

She was, perhaps for the first time in her life, fully in the moment. Not in the past, not in the ever present, entirely too detailed memories that made her who she was.

Suddenly, she was lifted away from him, brought up onto his lap, and they were kissing. Fiercely. He was untethered. A man without a rudder, she realized.

It should maybe be terrifying, but it was the most exhilarating thing she'd ever experienced.

She was having sex with a stranger.

Well, she was *about* to.

She'd just had the most intimate part of him in her mouth.

And now he was consuming her. Claiming her for his own. And she had never wanted anything more.

Wicked. Wicked. Wicked.

And tonight it would be only a good thing.

Tonight she would let it carry her into her darkest fantasy.

Tonight she didn't care about rules.

Because this was it, so what was there to behave for?

He saw her.

He knew she was a con artist.

He didn't care. He wanted her anyway.

He put his hands on her hips again, lifted her so that her knees were on his thighs. Then he grabbed the edge of her underwear, and pulled them to the side, exposing the heart of her to his inspection. He moved his hands around to cup her ass, and brought her up against his mouth.

A short scream escaped her as he began to lick deep within her.

Each stroke of his tongue created a white-hot streak of pleasure that rioted through her.

He moved one hand down between her thighs, and stroked where she was wet and needy for him, pushing a finger deep inside her from behind as he continued to lick her. Suck her. Taste her.

She lost control of herself. Completely. And that was another new experience. Because she controlled everything. The way she breathed, the way she looked, every step she took.

She ground her hips against his mouth, sought more, and then he pushed a second finger within her and she let a raw cry escape her lips.

"Yes," she said. "Yes."

"You are a very bad girl, aren't you?"

He had seen her. Seen the fear that lived in her. Was she wicked? He thought so. And he loved it. Reveled in it.

Made her like it, too.

It was so good. So good, it nearly hurt.

He growled that against her sensitized flesh, and she could only tremble in response.

He continued to lick her, and suddenly, it was like the whole world fell away.

And she along with it. She unraveled, as pleasure rolled through her like a wave.

Her internal muscles tightened around his fingers, and she had to grip his shoulders to keep from collapsing.

Dimly, she registered that he was still mostly dressed, while she was undone and naked before him.

She was about to say something, but he stood, bringing her over his shoulder like a caveman, one hand gripping her ass firmly, the other around her knees as he carried her through the penthouse and into the bedroom.

He threw her down onto the bed, and stood away from her as he began to undress.

And she just lay there, legs splayed, still wearing high heels, watching as he revealed his glorious body to her.

He undid his tie, the buttons on his shirt, his cuffs. And her mouth dried as he exposed the hard, heavy ridges of muscle that made up his chest, his abdomen.

His body was covered in course-looking golden hair, and she had to bite her lip to keep back her cry of desire as he took off his jacket, shirt, pants. As he revealed every bit of his body to her. His muscular thighs, and that thick, glorious member.

She'd already come once, but she was ready for more already.

He moved over to her, and grabbed the front of her underwear, pulling them down her legs, and off completely.

Then he returned to her, kissing her ankle, the inner part of her knee, running his tongue along her inner thigh before moving back to the heart of her, and pushing his tongue deep inside her.

Her hips bowed up off the bed, and she nearly screamed his name.

He moved up, to her breasts, taking one nipple deep inside his mouth and sucking hard.

If this was debauchery, then perhaps she had always been made for it.

But there were worse things, she supposed. Worse things than being debauched. Worse things than being wicked.

Worse things than knowing that every detail of tonight would linger in her mind forever and ever and ever.

She would go have a quiet life after this. But not tonight. Tonight she would be loud.

He opened up the drawer of his dresser and took out a condom packet, tore it open and quickly rolled the latex over his arousal.

And then he moved back between her legs, hooking her leg up over his head before he thrust hard inside her.

She had not been prepared for that.

She gasped, pain tearing through her.

"What the hell?" he asked, frowning fiercely.

"I'm all right," she said, putting her hands on his lean hips and urging him to stay there. "I'm fine."

"You're a virgin."

"Not now."

He gripped her chin and held her face. "What game are you playing?"

"I'm not playing a game. We played that game already. And I won. But I *saw* you. The same as you did me. I haven't been able to forget. I just wanted tonight. That's all. I just wanted you to be the first one."

Maybe the only one.

She just wanted him. That cost her nothing to admit it because she would never see him again. All she would have was tonight. This beautiful, raw memory of tonight.

"I cannot give any more than this," he said.

"I don't want any more than this. I couldn't take any more than this. My father is a crime lord. I've spent the last few years running from him. Trying to make a new life for myself. Trying to make myself safe." She refused to bring Maren into this. It wasn't her sister's fault that she had decided to do this. "I won tonight. I made myself safe. I'm going to go off and have my life. But I just wanted this first."

"But I will make it a night you don't forget."

If only he knew.

If only he knew she would never forget, no matter what. Not one breath. Not one heartbeat. Not one moment.

But she was grateful that he would make it wonderful. He withdrew from her, and then pushed back inside, and the delicious friction made her wild.

She wrapped her legs around his lean waist as the pain began to recede, as need replaced it.

His thrusts became hard, less measured.

And she felt her arousal tightening within her.

Felt herself climbing toward that peak again. But this wasn't an unraveling.

This time, when she came apart, she shattered. It was violent, intense, her body gripping his hardness, drawing him deeper within her, and he responded with an animal need. His thrusts wild and hard. And when he lost control, she felt like she was staring into the center of the sun.

Because it wasn't only she who shattered. But he as well.

And in the aftermath of it all, they lay there together.

She wondered if she would have to leave. If it was time for her to go and find Maren.

"Stay there," he said, getting up and going into the bathroom.

He returned a moment later with a towel. "I

will get you cleaned. And rest with you for a moment. But if tonight is all you have…"

"Yes," she said, relief rolling through her. It wouldn't be just once. "Show me *everything*."

CHAPTER THREE

HIS FATHER WAS DEAD. He wasn't sorry about that.

He had, however, expected to feel triumph.

He'd won, after all. His father had died alone in a care home and he had survived him. Instead, he had felt smothered by a blanket of heavy black darkness. It hadn't been grief. He knew grief. It had been something worse.

Futility.

He had outlived his father. He had made sure the old man knew that the line would end with him, that the estate was no longer part of the family.

But on the other side of that had been...nothing. Nothing but a strange finality he had not anticipated.

It was like he could no longer find the man beneath the mask. He'd always imagined he'd be there, somewhere. Healed when his father died and yet...the closest he'd felt had been with her.

He had been utterly unlike himself, as had the desire he'd carried for her every day since. She had aroused something deeper in him. Something dark and intense. He'd never been like that with a woman before.

Then he'd gone back to himself. To the Ewan he put on every day along with his suit and tie. And now his father was dead.

Everything was still broken.

Or perhaps that was Jessie.

He hadn't felt anything like triumph since that night he had spent with Jessie.

Five months and he hadn't gotten the woman out of his mind. Not just because they were connected by her winning the estate.

Jessie...

He had lost the taste for everything since that night. For anyone else.

That she had been a virgin was a shock. A gentleman would have taken her just the once. Allowed her to recover.

He was not a gentleman. But even beyond that...his behavior hadn't been about playing into the idea that he was a debaucher. He'd been lost to it. To her.

With her, he'd found something gritty and dark within himself. He'd made demands of her, and she'd met them. It had felt like meeting an old friend, or perhaps just a part of himself long buried.

He'd been a child when he'd smoothed that charm over the top of his intensity, and so he'd never had the chance to connect it to sex and need and desire.

But they had.

He had taken her every which way. He'd bent her over the couch in the living room. He'd had her in the shower.

He'd tied her hands and pleasured her until she had begged for release. And he had refused her until she was sobbing.

It had been the single most intense night of his life. And it should've faded into that hazy pool of memory where he kept all sexual encounters.

But it had not faded. It had stayed there. Bright and determined.

Perhaps that spoke volumes about how jaded he had become. It had taken a virgin to show him something exciting. And now he could find no interest in anything else.

Or perhaps it had been that night.

That finality he'd felt having surrendered his title, the estate, severed his ties with that house and his father forever.

She had been a conquest. A victory. And he'd been hers.

The mutual desperation had been unlike anything he'd ever experienced before.

She had been like liquid fire in his hands. And she'd begged for everything. And he had given it. Over and over again.

He had left no part of her without his brand.

She might have been a virgin when she came to his bed, but she had left with no more firsts to be given. They all belonged to him.

Even now, sitting there thinking of it he grew hard.

Even now, she was the only thing that made him feel.

And that was a strange thing, given he had not managed to find excitement for a woman standing right in front of him in the months since.

This was, without a doubt, the longest stretch of celibacy he'd ever endured.

And he had certainly never imagined that he would endure it simply because of his own lack of interest.

But maybe that was to do with the death of his father.

The way it hadn't fixed the cracks inside him. The way he wasn't restored, and everything from the past was still past.

Nothing was changed.

He sat there in his office, a billionaire in his own right, free of the man who'd poisoned him, and asked himself what the hell he had expected.

That he was fixable? Now, after all this time?

He knew better than that.

Or perhaps he hadn't.

Perhaps somewhere inside him a scared little boy had thought he was slaying a dragon, when in reality a bastard of a human being had died and his death didn't erase the scars he'd left with his existence.

Idly, he found himself looking up the articles on when she had won the estate.

It had been quite the headline. Tabloid fodder, to be sure, but that was exactly what he'd wanted it to be.

Jessica Lockwood. Kincaid estate.

But what he saw was not what he had expected. As he sat there in his gleaming office, he felt fire ignite in his chest.

There was a brand-new article. Just from yesterday.

And there she was. His beauty. Jessie. Round with a pregnancy.

He curled his fingers into fists. It had to be his baby. It had to be.

They'd made love countless times that night, and he knew that there had been a point when desire had taken over everything, and condoms had become an afterthought.

Because she had ruined him.

Changed him.

She had made him into a man who didn't care about consequences or anything that happened beyond that night.

Was he more than the playboy that night—a man given over to hedonism without a care for how it impacted anyone?

Or less? A man who felt it down deep, who

wanted it, needed it. Who wasn't easily succumbing to temptation for the hell of it, but who had been beyond himself in the moment. Beyond anything but the need he felt for it.

And it had felt incredible.

But there was the consequence of incredible. Right there in front of him. A magazine article that could not be denied.

His child.

He had sworn that he would not carry on his bloodline. His family name.

He died thinking you wouldn't. He died thinking that you had surrendered the estate.

His blood was at the estate whether or not he acknowledged it.

Of all the tricks that could possibly have been played.

His child would be the heir whether he staked a claim or not.

His child.

His child.

A baby.

He pushed the intercom button on his phone. "Natalie," he said, barking his assistant's name. "Have the private jet ready to leave. I need to go to Scotland."

"Yes, sir."

His tone brooked no argument. He made sure of that.

Other than that, he could not think straight.

Jessie Hargreave was pregnant with his baby.

He had to see her.

As quickly as possible.

Even though doing that meant a trip into hell.

"I don't know how anybody got in here with a camera without us knowing."

Jessie looked up at Maren, who was pacing the length of the dining room.

"It's fine," said Jessie, not feeling fine in the least.

"You won't think so if our father finds us." Maren's eyes were round with fear and whenever Maren was afraid, Jessie wanted to protect her.

Maren needed to be handled gently, and Jessie had always known that. She was soft. A little pink marshmallow of a human who had to be gently coddled.

"He didn't find us when the first news stories were printed," Jessie pointed out.

And she had a security detail, reporting her father's moves and making sure they were safe.

Maren frowned. "Yes, but more is just tempting fate."

It wasn't their father that worried her.

"You know me, Maren," said Jessie. "You know I'm not going to let him get us. He thinks he's smarter than us because he made us and that will always, always be his downfall. I've always been better at a math equation than him. Always better at angles. And you? You…"

"Will feel an intense emotion at him?" she asked, blinking slowly, her face placid. She was being dry, but with Maren it was hard to tell. It was part of her *innocent creature* persona.

"What are Dad's weaknesses?"

"His ego. His dependence on wealth, and his aversion to hard work."

"Issues we don't share."

"You can come with me," said Maren. "In just a couple of months I get to take occupancy at the castle that I won. I'm going to be a princess. I'll keep you safe."

"On your country that literally spans only the width of the rock the castle is on?"

"Yes. I will."

"I'm a duchess," Jessie said, even knowing that her claim to the title was specious. She needed it in this moment so she was taking it. "I'm perfectly capable of protecting myself. And my baby."

Finding out she was pregnant had been… It had been terrifying. And she had kept it a secret from Maren for as long as possible. She felt guilty about that.

The night of the poker game, her sister had also won an amazing prize.

The castle, and all the money that went with

the place. It was a whole kingdom, really, even though nobody lived there full-time.

It was only that she had to wait several months to take up occupancy. And in the end, that had been good.

But at the time it had felt…suffocating.

Maren had suspected something the night of the game.

Because Jessie hadn't come back until morning, and by the time she did sneak back into their hotel room, in the same dress as the night before, the sun had begun to rise.

"We have a rule, Jessie. For a reason."

Maren looked tired, angry and wounded.

"I know."

"I won my game."

"That's great."

"You weren't there," Maren said, accusing.

"I had my own business to see to. I won an estate."

"I know that. Everyone was buzzing about it before I won my game, but you were nowhere to be found. You went off with him."

"It was our last night, Maren. It's done. It's over and finished, and there's no reason that we need to be worried. There's no reason to keep being so careful…"

"You're wrong, Jessie. There's always a reason to be careful. When you become careless, you become like Father."

"Well, maybe I am like our father."

Maren had looked immediately regretful.

"You aren't."

"I might be. Just a bit more wicked than you."

"It isn't wicked to desire a handsome man. But I just worry... I worry."

"I know you do. But all is well."

"You aren't hurt?"

"I just had about thirty orgasms. I'm fine."

All of that came back to haunt her when she missed her period. And then another. When she was forced to take that first pregnancy test, and when she opted to keep it a secret.

The first day she threw up in the morning was the day that she knew. The day that she knew she couldn't keep it a secret anymore.

"I'm pregnant."

Maren had simply nodded.

"I know."

Maren would have made the better mother. They both knew it. But Maren wouldn't be this careless.

"How?"

"Nearly imperceptible differences with your appearance. But noticeable all the same. Plus, you seem sad. What are you going to do?"

"I don't know."

She had kept right on not knowing until she had felt it was too late to make any sort of drastic decision.

Maybe she'd done that on purpose. For she was not an indecisive person by nature.

In general, she was extremely confident. Always knew what she wanted the minute choices were presented to her.

She had known that she wanted Ewan from the moment she'd seen him.

So she'd had him.

But she couldn't imagine a baby. And maybe that was the most difficult part. What a baby made by her and him might look like.

She couldn't fathom it.

And maybe in the end that was why she hadn't decided to end the pregnancy. Because it was a mystery. Because it was something she hadn't anticipated.

Because in many ways she had finally caught herself.

And anyway, what were they doing out here? They were starting a new life.

She had intended to go to school. To find something she wanted to study, a job she wanted to do. She was interested in so many things…

But she had all the money she could possibly need, and now she was going to…be a mother.

She wasn't entirely certain she was maternal. She and Maren had barely known their mother, and she had been deeply uninterested in them.

Their father was evil. She knew what *not* to be.

And again, perhaps that was why she thought

maybe… Just maybe it would be worth having this child.

Except now it was in the paper, and she wondered if *he* would see it.

He may not do anything.

He didn't appear to want children. He had given up the estate in the interest of disavowing his bloodline, after all. He hated his father.

As for her…

He was too much for her. On top of all of this, the reality of knowing she was going to be a mother, she couldn't take him on with it.

He did things to her. He made her feel things.

He made her feel beyond herself.

She was going to have to find a way to…feel. Just for the child. Just open herself up just enough to be what her baby would need. She couldn't have him anywhere in the vicinity when she was…open.

He saw too much already. She couldn't take the risk.

She had to be the best mother she could be— and she had no earthly idea how good that actually was.

She had deliberately avoided looking at any photos of him in the months since they parted. She didn't think she could stand to see him with another woman, and worse, if she did, she would never be able to get that out of her head. And at night she replayed the hours they'd spent together. He was so beautiful.

Her memories of him were so vivid it was like she could reach out and touch him.

As if she could feel it all over again.

He was red.

And so was wanting him.

It painted every day.

It was why he needed to stay away.

"We can go away to my castle," Maren said stoutly.

She was adorable when she tried to be the protector.

"No. This is my home. Mine. And if I have to hire a security detail to keep me safe, then I will do it. But I won this place. It belongs to me. Just like your castle belongs to you. We set out to make new lives for ourselves, and I'm doing it. I'm…" She decided it was time to say it out loud. "I'm going to be a mother."

"Oh, Jessie," said Maren, her eyes filling with tears. "Do you want that?"

"I don't know. But it's happening. At least it was because of something I did. Think of all the terrible things that we went through in our childhood because of what our parents decided for us. I went to bed with him of my own free will. I wanted him. I wasn't careful. I knew better. I realized that the time when… I knew he didn't get a condom. The last few times. I didn't care.

I didn't care about anything but having him. It's my consequence for my mistake. From the beginning I made mistakes with him. He's the only one who has ever affected me like that…"

"I don't ever want that," said Maren, looking away. "It sounds terrifying."

"It is," she said. "But it was wonderful."

"*One night*, and you're going to have a baby that you have to take care of for the rest of your life."

"In fairness, it isn't going to stay a baby forever," Jessie said, putting her hand on her stomach. "I really do need to see a doctor, probably."

"Yes. You definitely do. But thankfully, you have enough money to have private visits at your estate."

"Very thankfully."

It was the roar of an engine that broke the conversation. Not a car engine. The plane. They both startled.

And she ran as best she could to the back window of the sitting room, to look out at the vast field behind them. Just in time to see a sleek white plane disappear behind the rise of one of the hills. There was a landing strip back there; she knew that. One of her favorite parts of the estate was the horses.

And even though she had to be a bit careful riding, she had gone on very mild rides in the past few months, all over the grounds. And she had explored what was obviously a place for planes and helicopters to land, plus a few other spaces that spoke to the wealthy excess of the previous owners. She knew. Immediately.

"He's here," she said.

"Father?"

"No, Maren. It's the duke. Ewan Kincaid."

CHAPTER FOUR

As the plane touched down, adrenaline fueled Ewan's veins.

It was as if he was descending into hell, not down to the shocking green of the Highlands.

But this place was hell to him, and had been all his childhood, since everything had been washed in crimson and stained forever.

Destroyed forever.

He tried to push the images back. He didn't have time to dwell in the past. He didn't have the mental energy to devote to it. The past was the past.

Death was final.

As soon as the plane stopped, he stood. "Be quick about it," he said to the flight attendant, who began to open the doors.

This was not him, he knew. He could see it in the faces of his staff members. Had seen it from the moment he had asked for the plane to be procured.

Normally, he was affable. Easy. He was a playboy, after all. His business was pleasure clubs. And he knew that you caught more flies with honey than vinegar. And he preferred to apply his honey liberally.

But it had all left his body when he'd seen Jessie round with his child.

He'd only had one thought. To get to her. To get here.

Only then would he be able to make sense of it.

Only then would he be able to find a way forward.

He was not a man who sat still.

His father was entrenched in tradition. Frozen at an archaic point in time.

Medieval. And cruel.

The sort of man who would beat a little boy for daring to be frail enough to cry for his mother. A man who had a near wild-eyed commitment to the name, to the legacy. Who cared more for his dead ancestors than he ever would for his own living child.

Ewan had never wanted to be thus.

And he never had been.

But now he was close to it. Touching the edge of it as if he was putting his finger to a flame.

It pained him to know that he could understand his old man. But in this moment, he very nearly did.

Because what did he care for the comfort of

those around him when he felt as if he was being dismantled from the inside out.

He walked down the plane's stairs, to the staircase, and continued straight into the green.

He walked up over the rise, and could see the estate down below.

He was wearing custom-made Italian shoes. Not practical for moving across the soft ground here in the Highlands.

His suit jacket wasn't practical, either.

And they were suffocating him.

This place. God in heaven, this place. He hated it. It was as if there were hellhounds here. Lurking on the edges of the wood. His heart pounded hard, and then it was like he couldn't breathe.

With speed and efficiency, he took his jacket off. He cast it down to the ground, then bent down and untied his shoes. Both of them.

He left himself barefoot. It was practical because the ground was soft. It was not desperate.

Then he ran.

Toward the estate. Toward her.

Until she was in his sight, they would be nothing but this. This confusion. This jumble of sound inside his soul.

This fractured feeling.

Was it his child? It might not be. He had been her first. He had been the man to introduce her to pleasure, and so maybe he had awakened a hunger in her.

She had been an eager lover.

It was possible the baby belonged to some-one else.

Does it matter?

What manner of father could he be?

All he knew was pain in that relationship. A father and son.

He had spent his life avoiding attachment.

He had none.

He changed assistants at least once a year. The staff on his private jet never remained the same. His clubs were constantly in a state of flux, as clubs often were. The ambiance, the employees, all shifted continually.

And he didn't stay long enough to truly get to know anyone.

He had tried to the best of his ability to escape this place. This place. As his feet met with the damp ground, it felt as if it was mocking him. Bringing up pieces of his childhood. Of the pain there.

He had been left outside in the cold before. Unable to warm his feet as they sank into the soft grass.

Huddled in a corner of the property trying to find some shelter.

He had been beaten. Shut away.

Starved. His father had always been cruel. His grief had driven him mad.

Turned him into a sadist who hid behind a raft

of rules and a need to control, control, control the son he'd borne. To make him the perfect heir as he would be the only one, the only hope.

He did not seem to realize that the way he'd treated his heir could have killed him.

As if bleeding his own pain out onto his son might heal him in some way. Like draining the poison to Ewan would fix something.

So Ewan had decided to deny him in every way. He'd cut off the estate. He'd disgraced their name. He'd decided there would be no children.

It was what his father had deserved. And so how was there a child now? How was he *here*?

How was he here?

That thought propelled him to the back door of the estate.

And he was ready to kick the door down when it opened. And there she was.

She was wearing a red flowing gown that poured over her curves. The neckline was plunging, showing her overflowing breasts. And the rest of the gown was loose, flowing easily over that baby bump.

"I knew it was only a matter of time," she said, shaking her head.

Her hair was lighter now. A chocolate brown rather than the raven's wing from five months ago. She was no less beautiful. If anything, even more so, with her curves rounded by her pregnancy.

She was clearly unwilling to appear even the least bit surprised. That cool calculation of hers he'd seen at the poker tables was visible here.

That, at least, was the same.

Though when her eyes dropped down to his feet, she could not hide her shock.

"Have you had an accident?" she asked.

"Other than the one I'm staring at just now? No."

She ignored that. "Where are your shoes?"

"I left them to the fields."

With his coat. He realized then that might have been sort of a mad thing to do, but he wouldn't show her that he doubted his own sanity.

"All right, then. You might as well come in."

He could see her. Doing mental calculations. Trying to figure out just how she was going to manage this. How she would come out on top.

He could think of nothing. Could strategize nothing. Because his brain had ceased to function. He was there. Standing before her. And she was pregnant.

"The child is mine," he said.

He'd meant it as a question. It had come out a statement of fact.

"Oh, no," she said. "I mean, it *could* be. But it's actually nearly impossible to say. I have just had endless sex since last we met. So many lovers I can't even begin to—"

He'd thought that. Had the suspicion himself.

But when she did…

When she did it was clear to him it was a lie.

"I knew you would say that," he said. "It's not even a good con as cons go."

"But you can take it as the answer, if you want to," she said, looking at him. "I don't know who the father of my baby is. I've had far too many lovers to keep track of. It could be anyone's."

She was lying. She didn't have a tell. And that was the biggest tell of all. For if she had told the truth, he had a feeling she would look much more vulnerable. As it was, she was defiant.

But she was offering him a chance to walk away.

But he had no honor, no connection to family or blood. That was what she didn't understand.

He wasn't here for *honor*.

He'd had to see. Like some beast had possessed him. Because she was here.

Here and pregnant.

And it had driven him here even though he now had no idea what purpose he served.

"You and I both know that's a lie," he said.

She shrugged, as if she didn't care. "Suit yourself."

He'd walked into the estate, and felt an oppressive sense of cold fold itself around him. And right then he hated that he had decided to take his shoes off, because being in here with his feet touching the floor felt far too much like being at home.

And this was not his home.

She tossed her hair. "I don't know if you realize this, but I'm a millionaire."

He laughed. Because at least that jarred him out of the moment he had found himself sinking into. The thoughts of the past that were threatening to reach up and strangle him.

"I am aware, as you achieved that status in part by taking a substantial amount of money from me."

"That's incorrect. You *lost* a substantial amount of money to me. And this estate. I am quite well, and taken care of."

"I'm not here for *you*," he said. "I'm here for the child."

But his head was beginning to pound and the ghosts of this place hung thick around him, pressing in hard, harder.

"What could you possibly want with a child?" she asked.

"What do *you* want with a child?" And suddenly, everything crystallized for him. She was a con artist. Beautiful. The sexiest woman he'd ever been with, but a con artist all the same.

She was not fit to be a mother. Any more than he was fit to be a father.

One thing he knew, as he stood there in this

oppressive place, was that he could not consign a child to a life of misery.

But they'd made one.

The poison had done its job. It had spread.

He was looking at the devastation.

Not only was she having a child neither of them were fit to raise, she also seemed to not understand the danger such a thing could represent.

But he knew.

He knew all too well.

"I'm having the child," she said. "It's kind of out of my hands now."

"That isn't true, and we both know that."

"I've decided to have the baby. So. That's what I want with the baby. I'm having it. And I want to see where it goes."

This girl had no idea. She was treating this like it was nothing. Like it couldn't be the death of her.

"It isn't a poker game, Jessie. Pregnancy is dangerous. And that is only the shortest bit of this. You cannot simply have the child and see if it goes your way, and fold if it doesn't."

Color mounted in her cheeks. "How *dare* you? I've spent the past four months coming to terms with this. Deciding what I was going to do. Do you think it was easy? And now you've come and you questioned me and you're acting as if you've put more thought into this than I when we both know you could not have known about the child for more than a few hours."

"It's clear to me. I don't need months to think about it. The baby is mine."

"Again…"

"Liar," he said, his voice fierce. He took a step toward her, and he pressed his thumb against her lips. "This mouth is mine. That lying tongue is mine. You did not spend all those years of your life untouched because you lacked opportunity. What we had was different. And you would not have gone off into someone else's bed after. You know that."

"Do I?"

"Yes," he growled.

Why did it matter? Why did it matter to him that she'd been with no one else? If she had, he could walk away.

She let out a hard breath. "Why are you here? Because we both know that you don't want a baby."

"And you do?"

She shrugged. "No. And yet, like you it seems as if I'm having one. What is there to be done? What is there to be said?"

"You know that two dysfunctional humans can't combine to become a single functional parent. We will only make this worse if we are together."

"I'm not suggesting we be together. But perhaps we need to figure out how we might both…"

"What whole thing will two broken shards make?" he asked.

"I don't want to. I want a life that's mine. You don't want a baby. So why can't you leave?"

She was offering him freedom. He wanted her.

But the idea of a child...

He could think of nothing worse.

Because all he could imagine was that night. The moment that changed everything. Destroyed it all.

A pale, still woman, and a baby that never cried.

Why was he here?

He could not endure it.

She would be better off without him. Because he was entirely tangled up in the monstrous legacy of this place, and the loss that happened here. The pain after.

And fathers with demons were nothing but devils.

He knew well enough that he could be Satan himself if the wind turned wrong. How could he deny it?

It was in his blood. Perhaps that was the best reason of all for his mask. For cutting off all that he'd been as a child.

Maybe his father had hated him so much because it had been like looking in a mirror.

Blood he'd been intent on cutting off. Blood that he...

But she was here and he wanted her. He knew nothing beyond that. It was desire that had brought them here and desire was the one thing he could understand.

Why was he here?

For this.

And he found himself closing the distance between them.

Then he lowered his head, and pressed his mouth to hers.

CHAPTER FIVE

JESSIE FELT LIKE she was on fire. She wanted to cry, and she wanted to keep kissing him and never stop.

This was unconscionable. She couldn't allow herself to be...seduced by the father of her baby. While he was standing there in a fury.

Why not? The damage was done.

In so many ways, the damage was done.

Why couldn't she have him? Maren was here. In the other room. But if they went upstairs now, she wouldn't see them. And even so, she would just have to apologize for her continued weakness later.

She was weak for him.

But she had a feeling that he would leave after this, because she had given him means of escape, and he would take it. She couldn't blame him.

It would be the best thing. The best thing for both of them.

But she'd never felt what she did when she was with him. Not before. And she never would after.

More than that, she couldn't afford to. She had to let it go.

She had to.

But she needed him again. She needed to feel like that just one more time.

She'd lived so many years cut off from her feelings. Until him.

It was bright and terrifying and something she should run from. But not now. Not now.

"Have me," she whispered against his mouth. "Please. One more time."

"Yes," he growled.

She didn't know this man. She still didn't know this man. Pregnant with his child, at the mercy of his kiss yet again, and she didn't know him.

She didn't understand why he was here barefoot, or why he had given the place away to begin with. Why he had come at all, and why he would leave since he'd come all this way.

She'd known from the moment she'd met him that he was more than he seemed.

But there was even more than she'd seen.

He was broken somehow.

Tortured.

Hurt.

She hurt for him. For herself.

Why was he here?

But she wondered if he didn't know the answers to that question, either. Any more than she could answer why she'd decided to carry this child.

And so she simply let herself get caught up in his kiss. Consumed by it. By him.

He lifted her up with ease, her dress trailing behind them as he carried her up the stairs. Because of course he knew this place.

Of course he knew the way to the master bedroom that she called her own, and he found it with ease, kicking open the door and sparing it no examination as he closed it again and walked her to the bed.

The gown she was wearing fluttered around her as he placed her gently at the center of the mattress.

"I did not think I would find such a thing so arousing. But seeing you, round with my child… Knowing that I've made you this way…"

He had no idea. No idea the depth of it. He had made her this way. She'd gone twenty-two years without ever much thinking of sex. Just a bit, when she was alone in her bed.

But he had taken her and made her a creature of need.

He had changed her in so many ways, and she could only stare at him, at those eyes, and wonder if she had changed him, too.

This felt out of control.

It seemed like perhaps she had.

She truly wanted to believe it.

She truly did.

And so, as he began to undress himself with shaking hands, she knew that he was as undone as she was.

She watched as he bared that gorgeous, perfect body for her, and she knew a moment of shame, because he was still perfect. Rippling muscles and utter glory, while she was round and…

When he uncovered that most masculine part of him, all of her insecurity vanished.

He was hard for her. And the need in his eyes was like an inferno.

He reached down, gripped the top of her gown and pulled it down, exposing her breasts, and then he divested her of the rest of the garment, leaving her only in a pair of lace underwear, her belly round and *obvious*.

She had decided to get dressed up like a femme fatale because there was no way to avoid him, and anyway it was how she fortified herself when she ran a con. She had decided to meet him where he stood because she knew that there was no other real option.

She hadn't anticipated *this*. Or maybe she had. Maybe somewhere, deep down, this was what she had always wanted it to become.

Maybe it was what she needed.

They could come together again, and it would never be enough. She knew that. Because there was some kind of sickness in them.

Something that made them need each other like this.

It wasn't just sex for him; she could see that.

Because he was not happy to be here. He didn't want to want this, and somehow, that made her feel even more aroused. Because it made her feel even more special.

This thing between them had always been real. Specific.

It had never been simple sexual desire. It had always been something deeper.

They were powerless in the face of it even now. Even as they attempted to cope with this new reality. The pregnancy.

Even as he was angry. She didn't know at what. Not her. But at something. Some darkness that seemed to be pushing at him.

"Beautiful," he said, his voice a growl. "You are stunningly beautiful. And mine."

She wasn't his.

He was leaving.

And it hurt her more than she wanted to admit.

She'd told him the baby wasn't his so he would leave. So she could have her independence. She was fine.

She was fine.

She was fine.

She didn't need him.

But now she *needed* him.

He bent down and pressed his mouth to her stomach. She shivered.

And then he looked up at her, and she saw something so raw, so painful, in his eyes that she had to look away.

He cursed, low and harsh, and then lifted her, putting her on her knees, with a pillow beneath her to help brace her stomach. Then he put his large, rough palm against her ass and squeezed her, before moving her underwear to the side.

And he was inside her before she could take her next breath.

And she wanted to weep with it. Because it felt right. It felt like home.

It was all the memories of what had come before, but something new. Because the desperation between them was real.

Because this was a goodbye she didn't think they would ever say.

But each stroke brought them closer to the end.

She'd already thought they'd found the end. But no. They were having to do it again.

She would have his baby. A piece of him, always.

As if the memories weren't enough.

As if he wouldn't always be red. And everything she saw.

Everywhere she looked.

"Mine," he growled.

And it was that, that edge that pushed her right over.

"Ewan." She cried out his name as her orgasm broke over her, and he gripped her hips tight and followed behind, pouring himself inside her as he growled his pleasure.

Her cheeks were wet with tears, and her body was trembling.

"Go," she whispered.

"Jessie…"

"You're right. Neither of us knows anything about having a baby. And what are we going to find out together?"

"Nothing."

"Just go, and know that everything will be fine."

She was breaking. She needed him to leave.

If he would leave someday, he had to leave now.

He had to.

"If you can't handle things…"

"I'll get help. I promise. I can't have you here." Her voice broke. "I can't."

"I would stay," he said. "If I didn't think I would cause more harm."

"It's okay."

And he dressed, and left her there. And she thought that she was going to shatter. Into a million pieces.

A million ugly pieces. And she would never

get that image out of her head, either. Of herself breaking apart without him.

She had never really loved anybody except for Maren before.

But there was something with him. No matter how much she wished there weren't.

"Go," she said again. Because she had to save as many pieces of herself for her child that she could.

Because she couldn't keep breaking for him.

CHAPTER SIX

THE FOUR DAYS following his departure from Scotland were like hell.

He didn't compare it to hell lightly. He had lived in hell before. At that very estate. He had lived it that day his mother had died. The day that he had seen his younger brother. Cold and still.

Dead before he even drew breath.

Everything good he'd known had died that day.

He knew all about hell. Most assuredly that it was a place on earth. He did not doubt that for a moment. But being without Jessie... Having made the decision to step away from her and the child...

In this decision he'd discovered a new level of hell.

And when he'd descended into those depths previously it had been beyond his control. This was not.

He could change it. He had the power.

He was no longer a child held hostage in the Highlands. He had ascended on his own, taken his status and little else out into the world and built an empire not apart from his father—better—an empire to spite him.

He could go back.

But for what?

For her?

He'd had to walk away.

It was the only way to spare them both.

Because what lay on the other side of this…

He had gone to her because he had to see. Or perhaps because he'd simply needed to see *her*. It had been foolish.

But he had gone.

It was hell. But he'd been with her. He'd known he wouldn't stay.

She didn't need him.

She'd wanted him gone. She'd made that clear when she'd declared the child wasn't his.

Or perhaps she was just giving you a choice?

It didn't matter.

He had done what he'd had to. He had done what was best.

If he had thought for a moment that his presence in the life of his child would…

If he had thought for one moment that he could be of good. That he could do something good as a father. But the problem was he didn't believe in the benevolence of fathers in general.

You left her.

He had.

Unbidden, images of their last time together flooded his mind and infused his veins with fire. He'd made love to her again because he'd been unable to stop himself. Because when it had been clear she wanted him as he wanted her, he'd been powerless against it.

That weakness was why. It was why he had to turn away from her. It was too much like his father, and if there was even a chance this flame could take all he'd made himself and forge him into that monster, he had to deny it.

But he worried. About the baby.

He didn't know the woman. And what he did know was a concern.

The daughter of an infamous criminal.

A con artist.

And she would be raising his child. His blood. But what did blood mean?

He had seen his mother's blood. Staining the white sheets after she bled out. His blood, too.

But worse, he had seen his father's blood, and how it had turned following the death of his beloved.

His father had never been a particularly warm father. He had loved his wife, and that was it. She was much younger than he was, beautiful.

She'd had him, and for years after they had tried to have more children. She had been driven by her need for more children, and his father had never seemed to care one way or another whether

Ewan was there or not. He was an heir. A convenience as far as passing down the family line, but that was all.

He meant nothing more.

But his mother… His mother had loved him. Being a mother had been her proudest achievement. She had put it above being a wife, and Ewan hadn't been able to escape the truth that his father had resented him slightly for that always.

But he had also loved his wife, and lived to give her what she wished. So they had tried for more children. Baby after baby.

Lost.

Most in the very early stages.

But finally, when Ewan was eleven, she had managed to carry one to term.

They'd had the very best doctors brought in. His father hadn't trusted that she would be safe in a hospital. He wanted total control over the environment. There had been high-tech medical equipment, and entire teams of people. But everything had gone horribly wrong, and to this day, he didn't fully understand what or how. It had been like a scene from the past. They hadn't been able to stop her bleeding. Not with anything, and at the same time, the baby had been in grave distress.

And she had been begging. Begging that the child be saved. And when it was clear the baby would never breathe, he was convinced that she had just chosen to slip away.

It was the moment when she had stopped fighting.

The very moment.

And then she had been gone.

And he had watched it all unfold. A frightened boy crying in the corner.

His father had railed against the medical team, and then had clung to his wife's body, wailing.

The baby was an afterthought. Lying there still and blue.

He had filled Ewan's vision. This boy who would have been his brother. Who had taken his mother from him. The fury and despair that had filled him with equal measure was a shattered, sharp memory. One that robbed his lungs of air even now.

He would never forget it.

He would never not be marked by that. Or all that had come after. The truth was that the poison had always been in his father's veins.

The loss of his wife had let it flow unchecked.

All the rage his father had ever carried over Ewan taking his mother's focus away had poured itself out on him. And the need to correct what he saw as softness in him.

And everything to do with babies and pregnancy... Ewan couldn't fathom ever facing such a thing. Above all else, he had yet to see why a child might need a father. He had needed a mother.

But she had died.

His child would have his mother. And no other poison.

You don't know that. You don't know what manner of parent she'll be. You don't know her. She is a woman whose arms you spent a pleasurable few hours in.

He couldn't imagine Jessie being cruel.

Why? Because she gave you her virginity? Because you think that makes her pure in some fashion?

No. That wasn't why.

She hadn't tried to bleed him for more money. She hadn't tried to exploit the fact that she was carrying his baby.

Yet.

And perhaps the issue was there was a bigger fish. A mark that she had in mind. She'd said she'd had other lovers. He didn't believe her. But maybe he should.

He growled, sweeping his papers off his desk.

He should go to one of his clubs. Find a woman interested in performing a scene and have her there in front of everyone.

He wasn't opposed to such things. No act was off-limits for him. Provided everyone involved was willing.

But he just…

He couldn't. Not as long as the memory of her skin beneath his hands haunted him in this way.

He stood up, realization pouring through him.

He would have to go back.

That decision was made and he was moving before he had a chance to fully process all of it.

He *couldn't* stay away from her.

He couldn't stay away from the child.

To what end?

At what cost?

He would hold her at a distance. Just because he was with her didn't mean he had to touch her. Perhaps there was a middle ground?

It nearly made him laugh.

He was not a man who knew a middle ground.

He burned bridges to ash and laughed at the destruction.

It was important to him to be confident in what he did, always. When he had broken away from his father, from his family name, he had been determined that he would make something new. And even if it was partly just to spite his old man, it had been his and his alone.

And now there was her. She had brought him back to the estate, a place he swore he would never go again, and he had gone back.

And here he was, poised to go back again.

The intercom in his office came on. "Mr. Kincaid, there is a woman here to see you."

Jessie filled his mind. Only Jessie.

"Send her in."

A few moments later the door to his office opened. The metallic disappointment he felt when he saw it was a redhead, and not Jessie, was disorienting.

"Mr. Kincaid," she said, bobbing into a quick, ridiculous curtsy. "Your Grace."

He lifted his chin. "I don't answer to that title anymore."

He'd given it away, even if it had only been a public showing of frivolity and nothing of weight.

The pretty redhead advanced on him, her brows low, her lips making a snarl. She was like a very mad kitten. "You abandoned my sister. And she needs you. *We* need you."

"Ms. Hargreave, I don't have the time…"

She leaped forward, and she pushed him with the edges of her fingers. It actually hurt a bit. "Don't act like I should care about your time! Our father found us. Please, Mr. Kincaid, she's too proud to tell you, but we need your help. You need to protect her. You need to protect your child."

Jessie had been looking into the cost of a personal security detail ever since she'd gotten that phone call out of the blue from their father.

"Aren't you going to congratulate me on becoming a grandfather?"

The ice that had dripped down her spine…

She was terrified. And Maren was even more terrified. She had begged Jessie to call Ewan back, but she couldn't do that. Her sister didn't understand. She was a virgin. She didn't know what it cost her to even think about Ewan. That in the days since he had left her she...

She had been altered, forever, by the passion between them, and she simply couldn't cope with having him near, not again. Only to have him leave.

Yes, she had promised that she would let him know if she needed him, but she wasn't entirely confident that she did.

It was unsettling that her father knew where she was.

But she had no real evidence that he wanted to hurt her.

It was far more likely that he would wish to manipulate them into working for him again. Using his connections and their past misdeeds to make enemies for them.

Their minds were incredibly valuable, and while he possessed the same sort of mind, three were better than one.

Maren had vanished yesterday, with a cryptic comment about getting help herself.

Fine. Maybe her sister's new palace and title would get her what they needed.

Maren was going to be a princess.

That had to hold some weight.

She stood up and went to the window, looking out over the vast green.

And then she felt a flutter in her stomach.

She put her hand there. "Baby? Is that you?"

Could she really feel her child moving?

She was stunned by that.

And then gripped with a vicious feeling of protectiveness.

"If that bastard comes after us, I'll kill him. And I will relish the memory of it. The one that will never go away. Because it won't."

But her baby being like her? It made her want to weep. For the first time, she thought of the baby as a person. Not a circumstance that had been imposed upon her, but what would be a human being, independent of her. Walking around in the world.

"I don't want to hurt you," she said. "But I'm afraid. I don't know how to be a mother. I don't know how to be anything but a con artist. I was never taught anything different or better. Your aunt Maren and I were taught nothing about how to love. About how to be a family. We were only ever taught how to use people. But I want you to learn better. She and I have learned how to care for each other. To put each other first. We'll do the same with you. She'll help me. And anyway, she's a princess. Which is pretty cool."

And just then, she saw a white plane descending. There was no doubt what that meant.

"No," she said.

He was here.

She couldn't bear it. She couldn't bear to be confronted by him, not at this moment. Except…

Maren.

This was Maren's doing.

"I take back everything that I just said. Your aunt Maren is a turncoat. She's… She's not to be trusted."

She grabbed her phone and called her sister. *"Maren,* what have you *done?"*

"I'm making you safe," said Maren.

She could hear commotion through the phone. Likely the opening of the plane door.

"I told you not to involve him. He doesn't want anything to do with me or the baby."

"That isn't what he told me."

"Hey."

"Jessie," and she would know that voice anywhere. "You have no choice. This is exactly the kind of thing that you said you would tell me about."

"I have assessed the risk and determined that it does not require you or your intervention."

"It requires me."

"It doesn't."

She heard a car door close. "I will not watch you bleed out and die, do you understand me? I will not lose you or this child. I will brook no argument on the topic."

"You have no authority over me," she said.

"I am the Duke of Kilmorack. And I will exercise the authority in my blood."

Fury filled her. "*Technically*, you gave the title to me."

"*Technically*, you can't do that." And then he hung up.

She growled in frustration and flung her phone down onto the couch.

She knew they would be here in only a couple of minutes.

Now she was afraid, and angry and she didn't know which was worse.

She paced back and forth, the length of the room. And didn't stop moving until she saw a black town car pull up in front of the estate. She could see her sister and his Royal Dukeness sitting in the back.

They got out of the car, and she was struck by the way Ewan towered over Maren. He was such a tall man. And he looked good walking next to her sister.

She fought back a wave of jealousy. What a ridiculous thing.

She had no claim on him. She didn't want one anyway.

And Maren certainly didn't want him.

It was just that they were both very beautiful. And together, even more so.

She swallowed down that surge of ridiculous anger and walked downstairs to the vast entryway of the estate.

Her home, which was supposed to be a place of tranquility. Instead, it had been nothing but drama.

It's not the house's fault that you decided you needed to jump Ewan after winning it from him.

No. She supposed not. And in the end, the pregnancy was why all this was happening.

Her own lack of self-control.

It wasn't fair. She had been controlled all of her life.

She had never made a mistake.

Except this very tall, very handsome, mistake that was spidering out of control into lots more mistakes.

When the front door opened, she was standing there with her arms crossed tightly over her chest.

"And what exactly do you think you're going to accomplish by being here?"

But then his stormy eyes were on her, and he was moving toward her with purpose.

With single-minded intent.

He reached out and grabbed hold of her, pulled her against his body. "There is no question about what happens now, Jessica. Your father knows where you are. You owning this estate isn't going to insulate you from that fact. You need something stronger. You need my name."

"I need… What?"

"My name. You will be the Duchess of Kilmorack, Jessie Hargreave. You will be my wife."

CHAPTER SEVEN

HE HAD KNOWN this was the only real option from the moment Maren had told him what was happening.

Hell, he had been on his way to that conclusion anyway.

He had been ready to board the plane back to Scotland even before he'd found out there was a real threat of danger.

And he did not doubt that he would've decided *this* before it landed.

Maren had simply crystallized it all.

He could sense her vibrating with barely contained anxiety behind him.

"I'm sorry, Jessie…"

"Don't tell me you're sorry. You did this on purpose." Jessie in a fury was a sight to see. He'd seen her passionate, and he'd seen her contained, playing a role. He had not seen this. This uncontained, incandescent rage. "Why couldn't you just listen to me? Why couldn't you let me handle it? You're always so cautious, Maren. If it wasn't for me, we wouldn't have any of this. I'm the one that led us through. You had all your *stupid rules* all the time. And maybe if you hadn't been such a prude, maybe if you hadn't insisted that we not touch any man, I wouldn't have lost my mind over this one." She jabbed her thumb toward him but didn't look his way.

He looked between the sisters. "Is that true? Did you have rules?"

Maren looked up at him in a beseeching way. "Well, yes. We have… Has she not explained this to you?"

He looked down at Jessie, his *lover*. The woman who was carrying his child. The woman he knew almost nothing about. "I know that your father is a career criminal. A dangerous man. I know that you are both con artists."

Maren sniffed. "We are not. We *were* women experiencing con artistry."

"Is that a thing?"

"Seems more fair. I don't think *con artist* is what we want to be defined by."

He turned narrowed eyes to Jessie. "And you?"

"I can own it." Her own eyes glittered, all the rage simmering there multifaceted, like a particularly sharp jewel. "Con artist fits. Why not use it?" She turned away from him, clearly wanting to put distance between the two of them.

"Other than that," he said, looking back at Maren. "I know very little about her."

"She's a genius, you know. We—"

"You're card counters. I know that. I actually saw you both months before the last poker game. While I was building up to losing my family estate and titles."

"You're kind of a con artist yourself," said Maren.

Jessie whirled around. "He is *absolutely* a con artist. And a coward. You had every opportunity to claim me the last time you were here and you walked away. So now what? Now that you get to play the part of Batman you're happy to storm in? Now that you get to be the night, and vengeance and whatever else, owning up to the fact you knocked me up is cool enough for you? You didn't want to marry me then."

If she was remotely close to the truth it might have made him angry. But she wasn't.

"I can't say that I want to marry you *now*," he said. "But it has become a necessity. The truth is, Jessie, if I thought for one moment that my presence would have added something to the life of you or the child, I would never have left. But listen to me now. I am not the hero of your story. Not then, and not now. However, now… Now I know that you need me. Now I know that you need me to keep you safe. The scales have balanced. My absence is now more harmful than my presence. And that's why I'm here."

"I have done a damned good job of protecting myself. Protecting us for all this time. I don't need you."

"I'm afraid that we do," said Maren. "And if you're willing to take the chance with us, that's fine, Jessie. We've always taken chances by ourselves. But the baby…"

"Don't talk to me about the baby," said Jessie. "The baby is mine. Mine. You," she said, turning to face him again, "were ready to leave us."

"I was on my way back before Maren came."

"I'm going to leave you two to talk," said Maren.

"Coward," said Jessie, her eyes narrowed.

"Maybe," said Maren. "But mostly, this isn't my fight."

"You *made* it your fight," said Jessie.

"No. I just brought in the person that you should have been discussing this with all along."

Once Maren was gone, Jessie rounded on him.

"I'm not going to marry you."

"Don't be a fool, Jessie. What is the point of having this estate? What is the point of having this life if it's under threat?"

"You don't want this."

He wanted her. That much was clear.

But… He did not possess the capacity to be a husband. He did not see what benefit he could be as a father.

"My name will protect you. And while we

work to ensure that your father is put behind bars, you need that name."

"My father, behind bars? Do you really think you can accomplish that? Many have tried and failed."

"I have never failed at a single thing that I've ever put my mind to. I don't intend to start now."

"So confident. For a man who ran from here only a few days ago."

"Every decision that I've made so far has been about what I thought would be better for the child. Believe me when I tell you, there are worse things than having no father."

She looked at him, that luminous green boring into his soul. "You think I don't know that? My father is the person creating all these problems now. Of course I know that. But you..."

"What? You think because we have incendiary sex we can make something more of it?"

"Not anymore. Because I already know who you are. You walked away from me. For five months, you were away from me. You knew where I was. And then you came back, and you saw that I was having your child, and you left again."

"You told me to leave," he said.

She jerked backward as if he'd struck her. "A gentleman wouldn't remind me."

"I am not a gentleman." He moved toward her. "We are strangers, Jessie. Nothing more than two people who found pleasure in each other's bodies. That does not make us fated. But if you need some things explained to you, then I will do so. I never wanted to return here. This was a house of suffering. Why do you think I hate my father? Do you think it was because he would not increase my allowance when I asked? Do you think that I'm a poor little rich boy? Is that what you suppose? My father was a monster. He starved me. Beat me. Neglected me. Under the guise of making me stronger. Because the weak perish. And I would either become strong or die. He would see his line carried on by an honorable man, one like him who never turned a public scandal." He grinned. "So I became public scandal."

The color drained from her face. "But you... You were his son..."

"Yes. But he was mad. And you cannot reason with a madman. Or an evil one. So believe me when I tell you, I have no interest in attempting to do so with your father."

Her throat worked. The evidence that she was affected by what he'd said written in the paleness of her skin.

"It will be a marriage in name only, and I will be here until I'm certain you're safe. I cannot ever be a real father to the child. Do you understand that? I can never be a real husband."

She glared at him. "I don't want you to be."

"You seem angry about me leaving."

"It's complicated, Ewan. I don't like feeling abandoned, and I don't like feeling manipulated and all of it's happening all at once. I have to be a mother, and I don't have the energy for you, but I hated that you left even though I asked you to. I am pregnant, my father is a narcissistic sociopath and I refuse to be reasonable because I feel I deserve an outburst!"

He reached down and gripped her chin, and regretted that the moment his thumb and forefinger made contact with her soft skin.

"I'm sorry," he said. "That things are this way. That I am this way."

She looked away. "So tell me, how many times a year do you have to deal with something like this?"

"Never. I'm always careful."

"You weren't careful with me."

He shook his head. "No. I wasn't."

"You admit it."

"How can I deny it?"

She shook her head. "I don't want you here. I don't want to marry you. I don't want you to be high-handed and…"

"It has to be a big wedding, and it has to happen soon. It must be visible. You must, for all the world, be the wife of Ewan Kincaid. Do you know why?"

"Yes. Because coming for me will be visibility

my father won't want. But as long as I'm nothing and nobody squirreled away in the Highlands…"

"Exactly." He looked at her. "You're not a foolish woman, Jessie. You did not get where you are by denying reality. You and I both know that."

She tilted her head to the side, as though she'd just had a realization. "It's a con."

"If that makes you feel better."

"It makes *sense*. My father is nothing more than a con artist willing to shed blood. He fancies himself some kind of a mastermind. But it isn't anything quite so exciting. He's a petty con man who started killing people. That's it."

"Why does he want control of you?"

"We are strangers. You don't need to know that."

And with that she turned and walked away, leaving him standing there in the entryway of this house that haunted him in so many ways.

CHAPTER EIGHT

JESSIE HAD THE door locked firmly, as she sat in her tepid bath, angry that it couldn't be hot for the safety of the baby, and angry at her sister, and Ewan.

The firm knock on the door jolted her.

"I'm sorry," said Maren.

"No, you aren't."

"I'm sorry that you're mad at me. I'm not sorry about what I did."

She craned her neck to hold her chin above the water. "Then your apology means nothing."

She felt bruised. What he'd said about this place, about his father. Mostly because it made what he'd done somewhat understandable and she didn't especially like that.

She didn't want to humanize him. He was right. They didn't know each other. And she felt strongly that perhaps they shouldn't.

"I didn't know what else to do."

"Well, Maren," said Jessie. "What you could've done is at least talk to me. At least…"

She sighed heavily and got out of the bath, wrapping herself in a towel.

She stepped over to the mirror and looked at herself. She looked exhausted.

She had been sad and miserable ever since Ewan had left here four days ago, and all of this was only making it worse.

She went over and unlocked the bathroom door, then turned back to the mirror again. There was a firm knock again.

"Well, come in," she said.

Except when the door opened, it was Ewan.

She gasped and took two steps away from him.

"You said to come in."

"I didn't know it was you. I'm naked and soaking wet."

He lifted a brow. "You've been naked and soaking wet beneath me on multiple occasions."

Heat consumed her and that just made her angry. "You know what I mean. That was beneath you."

"You have been…"

"Stop."

"You are the one who needs to stop."

His tone was grave, his eyes on her body far too keen. And she felt as if he could see straight through the towel. He might as well be able to. He had seen her, after all. She had no shame with him, no self-control. If she could take back any one thing—other than giving herself to him that first night—it would be the way that she had surrendered to him when he had come just days ago. When he had left her.

You pushed him away. You didn't want him. And he was happy for the excuse.

It was true.

They had both been searching for ways not to deal with each other. And they had both been happy to take the reasons they had found.

And now things had changed. And she was loath to admit it.

She wanted to solve the problem. Because she always solved the problem.

Maren was the dreamer. Maren saw things in ways that Jessie often couldn't.

But Jessie made the plan.

If Maren dreamed it, then Jessie articulated it.

Mind palaces and file folders. That was how they were different.

And she had to admit, even if privately now, that if Maren couldn't see a way out of their current situation, even with her dreams, even with her more naturally optimistic personality, then there was no way out.

It would be great to get their father arrested, but complicated. They knew there were a few of his men inside law enforcement and they'd agreed it was a bit too risky. They could find themselves back at the compound or in a cell.

No way in hell.

She hated that. Hated that truth with a passion, because the man standing before her was likely her salvation.

"Speak now, then," she said, trying to sound imperious.

"What did your sister mean?"

"By what?" she said with an exasperated breath. "My sister has said a lot of nonsense today."

"About you. Your mind."

She looked at him from the side of her eye. "We're card counters. You know that."

"It isn't that simple, though, is it?"

She decided then that not answering would just make him more interested. And she'd rather have him cheerfully skip off to Narnia.

So the truth it was.

"It's an eidetic memory. Not the most extensive ever recorded, but it's a lot. I can often remember what happened on a precise date. I can recall with perfect detail situations that I was in. Maren and I spent a lot of time training ourselves. So that we were not bombarded constantly with unfettered memories. You have to keep them in files, you see."

"Really?"

He looked at her like he was interested. Not like she was a specimen, and she found that was different and notable compared to the way many people looked at her, especially men.

But even more surprising, it made her want to talk to him.

"Yes. That's how my father has grown his crime empire. He has the same kind of mind. And he has designs on ours. We were tools to him. That's why we ran away. We decided we wanted a different life. And that is also why we decided there was an endpoint on the con. We were made to be grifters from birth. We didn't choose that. But using those skills, we decided to find a way out of that life."

"He doesn't want you out."

"No. At least, that's the concern. And I don't want anything hanging over my head. Or Maren's. Or the baby's. The baby most of all. Maren and I didn't ask for this predicament. But... The choices I made are why I'm pregnant."

"The choices I made, too. So let me help you."

She felt her expression get petulant along with her tone. She couldn't help it. "You left."

"And you're upset about it now."

"I'm upset... I'm upset at myself. I'm upset about everything. I lied. Okay? I'm a good liar. I lie easier than I do other things. I lied to protect myself. I lied to myself. I told myself it would be easier if you weren't there, but it hurt me that you rejected the baby. It hurt me that you wanted to take the excuse."

He stared at her for a long moment, and she

felt exposed. "Jessie, what do you suppose this is? What do you suppose can be made of this?"

She knew she was inconsistent. But she'd never been pregnant before. She'd never had a lover before. It was confusing. All of it.

She wanted him here, but she did need some boundaries. Badly.

"It isn't about me. It's about the baby. I don't want you to reject your child." She suddenly felt tired, and soggier than she would like. "Can we step out of the bathroom, please? I don't need to have maidenly modesty in your presence, but I do want to get dressed. I'm starting to get chilly."

Unfortunately, she did feel a measure of maidenly modesty; she just didn't want to demonstrate it to him. So as soon as she exited the bathroom, she let the towel fall to the floor and walked with as much cool as she could muster to the closet, where she disappeared inside before selecting an outfit.

She'd ordered a great many loose and flowing things.

And leggings that stretched infinitely. She emerged again a moment later with a very large sweatshirt and some of those very leggings.

"Sorry. It isn't exactly the clothing of a seductress." She did a small shimmy for effect.

But he was staring at her, and she could see the heat in his eyes.

He should have laughed at the shimmy.

He hadn't.

"No. If I agreed to marry you for the sake of the baby, for protection, we have to have very clear ground rules. You and I do not play well together."

"The problem with you and I is that we play rather too well."

She sighed. "But we can't just have sex constantly."

"Agreed, but I'm curious. Why do you feel that way?"

"Because it cost me too much. Because I remember everything. Don't you understand that? Everything. Every detail. That's why we had rules. That's why we could never take lovers. Because of this. Because when I think about that night it's a film that plays in high definition in my mind over and over again, and I can't stand it. I can add to it. I can't... I'm not in love with you. I don't want to be. I don't think I could be. I don't want to be obsessed with you, either. It isn't fair. It isn't right. I want more for myself than that. I want to have this new life. I want to have it on my terms. Being forced to do anything because of my father is unconscionable to me. But I acknowledge that this is out of my hands. Out of my control. But I won't... I can't. Not again."

"You will have to marry me. And at as public a venue as possible. It will have to be a story. About that poker game. About that passionate night. It will need to seem as if we are madly in love. Because your father has to believe that there is a wall around you so protective, he cannot cross it."

"He won't care…"

"He will. And if it doesn't work, then he'll be entrapped. Because I will have men set around you. I will keep you safe, Jessie. I promise you. I will keep the baby safe."

He lowered his head. "I don't have a high opinion of fathers."

"Neither do I. For obvious reasons."

"I do not know what I can offer this child. I don't know what I can give. But what I know is that there is a graver sin and that's not offering protection now when I could."

"I think that I would be fine if…"

"No. We have to make it impossible for your father to come at you. We have to make you safe. It is paramount that we do so. It is essential. And if I were to stand by and allow him access to you and something were to happen to you, I would never be able to forgive…" He shook his head. "I do not need forgiveness or redemption. But I need you safe. And the baby."

"Why?"

She was truly baffled by it. He had been willing to walk away from her, to accept that she was able to take care of herself on her own before her father had been introduced into the equation. He had felt no particular loyalty to her then, and no draw to the child. So why now? Why had this made a difference? She truly didn't get it. She wasn't someone with an innate moral compass. She could acknowledge that.

She was all right stealing from people as long as they were the right sort of people to steal from. She had been totally fine having sex with him when he was a stranger. She hadn't been a virgin out of any sense of moral obligation to purity or treating sex like it was special. Her morality was fixed by being raised by a criminal. And otherwise, it was based on largely not wanting to cause harm. But in a blanket sense. She didn't have the impression that he was much more keyed into honor or morality than she was. So what the hell?

"I cannot and will not allow you to be harmed," he said. "That's all you need to know. Because in my mind, there is a very thin line between a man that actively harms those in his care and a man who allows harm to occur because he does not act. This place is hell to me. I will not allow it to become hell for you. Do you understand me?"

It made her feel small and somewhat wounded. And she had no idea why. She did not expect anyone but her sister to truly care about her. She didn't expect Ewan to care.

But it was far too easy for her to think back on the night they'd spent together, and the time here in the estate. His hands on her skin. His lips on hers.

To feel like that must have been caring.

It wasn't.

It never would be.

"So you feel…obligated?" she asked.

"Yes, I feel obligated. I might as well jump out of the highest window of this house if I cannot bother to put myself to use keeping you safe. Can you understand that? My life would be forfeit, and I would be nothing. No amount of money can erase such a sin. No amount of power. There is nothing worthwhile on this planet that a man could claim if he fails those around him. When they are most vulnerable."

She blinked, uncertain when tears began to fill her eyes, only certain that they had. He had so much conviction in that statement, and sometimes she was afraid she lacked conviction. She liked to win. She didn't know much else about herself.

"You said you don't know me."

"I can get to know you."

"Can you? When you do, will you let me know who I am? Because I don't know. I'm still trying to figure it out. I'm still trying to decide. When I was born, I was nothing but clay for my father to mold, and the problem with a memory like mine is you don't forget anything. So I remember all of his lessons whether I want to or not. Everything that he ever taught me about how I have to look out for myself. And now I have to figure out how to be a mother. Isn't that essentially caring for someone else more than you do yourself? I was never taught that."

"We'll begin by letting me care for you."

She stood there for a long moment. And she realized that if there was even a chance that her father might hurt her, and she had turned down his protection... If she had the opportunity for him to intervene and she hadn't taken it, and the baby was used against her... She would never forgive herself. And that was an introduction to a new thing about herself.

"I'll marry you," she said. "Until the threat of my father is neutralized."

"Well then, you best get prepared. Because this isn't just going to be a wedding. This is going to be a whole Cinderella story."

"I've never wanted to be Cinderella."

"Who did you want to be?"

"The fairy godmother. She's an independent woman who can turn a pumpkin into a carriage. All Cinderella could do was get the attention of a prince when she was wearing enchanted clothing. I want to be the one who does the magic tricks."

"That's an interesting way to look at it."

"You heard a little bit about my childhood. *Interesting* is the only way I can look at anything."

"We will put a marriage announcement in the

paper today. I will alert the media. We will marry in two weeks' time."

"Two weeks?"

"You object?"

"That's hardly time to plan anything."

"Suddenly you care?"

How strange. She sort of did.

"Not really. I never thought that I would get married. I'm not especially attached to the idea, but you know if I'm going to have a wedding, maybe it should be kind of pretty."

She had not realized that she possessed even the slightest bit of a romantic bone in her body. She thought that was entirely Maren's territory. And here she was, saying things like that about a wedding.

"You know what," she said. "I only care because there are going to be pictures of me everywhere."

"I don't believe you."

"Well, what about you? Did you ever think you would get married?"

"No. I very much intended not to. But my father didn't live to see the day, so I suppose every cloud has a silver lining."

"Indeed. How nice to be a cloud."

"A sexy cloud."

"A cloud that you aren't going to touch."

She didn't know why his compliments affected

her. Men had always called her beautiful. Sexy. It didn't mean anything to her because they didn't.

And that right there was a troubling revelation. Ewan was a playboy. He was used to complimenting women. He was accustomed to flattering them. It meant nothing. It meant *nothing*.

And she meant just as little. He wanted to protect the baby.

But still… No one had ever been protective of her other than her sister. And they were more protective of one another.

But the sensation of wanting someone to protect her, even if it was because she was a vessel for the actual main attraction… It did something to her. She didn't want to admit it, but it did.

This was just so damned difficult. And complex.

But she was smart. She hadn't gotten this far being emotional, and she wasn't going to start now.

You're going to have to be something for the baby.

Well, yes. But she had months to figure that out. So… She would take months.

But she only had two weeks to think about the wedding. And the fact that she was going to be a bride. She only hoped that she had the wits necessary to withstand him. She could make her brain work in her favor. She forgot nothing. And while she couldn't convince herself anymore that he was simply a vacuous playboy—there was more to him than that—it was the part he chose to play.

If there was one thing she understood it was that the commitment to a role could be stronger than the truth about someone's whole personality.

She knew because she lived it.

She knew because it was her.

And when the wedding came around, she would be smart. And when they got married, she would remember that it was only until she and the baby were safe.

Because they had created this accidental child together. And they would protect her together. She looked at him, and suddenly she felt resolved. Like the two of them might have something deeply in common.

Neither one of them had been protected by the people who should've protected them most.

And together, they would not allow the same fate to befall their child.

On that, they could agree. No matter what.

"Two weeks," she said finally.

"And it's going to be a hell of a party."

"Great," she said. "I love a spectacle." Though usually, she liked a spectacle because it was distracting from the con. And this was indeed a con, but she wasn't entirely sure it was a con designed in her favor.

But the thought of a con at least made her heart beat a little bit faster. It was a relief to have her heart doing that over something other than Ewan.

CHAPTER NINE

THE ANNOUNCEMENT HAD created a splash in world headlines, just as he had predicted that it would. Just as he had known it had to. But there was one more thing he felt he needed to see to before he would feel good about the direction they were taking things. Yes, he had private investigators working to find what evidence was required to take her father down. But the thing about Ewan was he was a man who did not intimidate easily. Or at all. When you were raised by the very devil, what could frighten you?

He shut the image out of a limp blue baby.

There was nothing to be scared of in the past. They were only memories. And he was doing his very best to make sure that those memories were not his future.

Or the future of the child who had not asked to be conceived. Let alone by two such broken people.

Broken though they might be, he was nothing if not bold.

And that was what brought him to her father's front. It was an office building, like any other. One could be forgiven for believing that it was actually a legitimate business. But of course, he knew it wasn't. He knew the authorities were well aware it wasn't, either, but so far the man remained untouchable. Whether because there was a labyrinth of crooked police officers or other more complicated reasons, he did not know. But he intended to find out.

He also intended to walk into the other man's office today and throw down a gauntlet of his own.

Because he knew that the other man would've seen the headlines.

And he knew that he would have been making plans.

Ewan intended to upend those plans.

He moved through the reception area, barely glancing at the secretary.

She wasn't there to check people in, after all.

There was a metal detector, of course. He was searched for weaponry when he got off the elevator. He was not so foolish as to bring a weapon into the building.

There may be a day when it came to that. But he would choose his venue. And it would never be on Mark Hargreave's home court.

"You have an appointment with Mr. Hargreave," the man waving the magnetic wand over his body said.

"No," he said. "However, he will know that we have a connection. Ewan Kincaid. Duke of Kilmorack."

"Indeed you do," said the man, proving that he was more than just a goon. He was someone who was privy to the conversation in his boss's office.

"Yes. And it is about the business that you would expect."

"Then he will look forward to an appointment with you."

"He doesn't even have to anticipate it. I'm here."

"You know he has many people hoping for an audience with him."

"But only one of them is the father of his first grandchild."

The man chuckled. "We'll see if he'll see you."

He disappeared behind the door and opened it a moment later. "He's feeling generous today."

"Just my luck," said Ewan.

His playboy charm was turned up to eleven, and he knew that it was likely to irritate the other man, so he made sure that his smile was brilliant.

He walked in as if he didn't have a care in the world. Much less a plan.

"Mr. Kincaid," said Hargreave from behind his desk.

He could see nothing of his daughters in the man.

Perhaps they weren't his. But then, if what Jessie said was true, they had his mind. But the girls were beautiful and petite, and this man had the look of a blunt instrument.

You could put a wild jackal in a suit, but that was what he remained. And Ewan should know. His father was of noble blood, for all that it meant, and he had still been a jackal.

A scavenging hyena that just wanted to pick the bones around him clean.

"I thought that we ought to become acquainted with one another. Since we are about to become family," said Ewan.

"You have something that belongs to me."

"By that, I suppose you mean your daughter? A bit old-fashioned, don't you think?"

He spread his hands over his desk. Shiny, glossy and wide. He was wearing a sharply cut suit. His American vowels were broad, out of place almost, and Ewan had a feeling Hargreave traded on that. "I'm a traditional man."

Ewan nodded. "And so am I. It's why the two of us are getting married before we welcome the child. I don't care, of course, and my love for her transcends such ridiculous notions as marriage. But I do want to do the right thing by her. Or the right thing by you."

"What do you want?"

"I want nothing. Except for you to stay away from my wife."

"She's not your wife yet. And she was my daughter first."

"She left. She doesn't want to be with you. I have to warn you that I take it very seriously and very personally if anyone makes what's mine feel threatened."

"It's funny. I was going to say that I take it very seriously and personally when somebody takes what's mine," said Hargreave.

"Again. Your daughter removed herself from your possession. She doesn't want to be in your life. And you will respect that."

"Do you think I couldn't have you all eliminated? You, the baby. My daughter is of some use to me, but the rest of you…"

Ewan fought back blinding, violent rage. He had to stay cool. Make it clear he was in control here. He could not let emotion lead him.

It was the strength of the emotion that shocked him. "Do you think I can't have the same done to you? And now if something happens it will be easily traced back to you. Isn't that the only thing keeping you here, in this office building? That plausible deniability. But now you've made threats, and I've heard them. And I will make sure that it's known far and wide unless you steer clear of us. I know that you're a powerful man, but you have no idea who I am. Not really. The whole world doesn't know who I am. But I'm happy to introduce them."

"A compelling speech. You are nothing and no one to me. A playboy billionaire."

"A member of one of Scotland's oldest and most important families. Descendent of the clans in the Highlands. Back then, I simply would've taken a broadsword and separated your head from your shoulders. We were given this land and title by the British. But I'm from Clan McKenzie. And it is rooted deep in our history and our blood to keep our women safe. Our children safe. And it suits me to have the world think of me as a playboy. Have you never thought of that? In much the same way it suits you to have the world believe that you're some sort of altruistic businessman. Someone who is always adjacent to dangerous things, but it can never fully be attributed to you. That benefits you for obvious reasons. But you've never stopped to ask if it might benefit someone else? Are you too much of a narcissist?"

"You're on dangerous ground."

"Unlikely. Since I own much of the ground. I could buy this out from under you tomorrow. You might have a criminal empire. Worth millions. I'm worth billions. Your fortune could be mine in mere seconds. At the snap of my finger. The only thing that could give you an edge on me is if I was not as ruthless as you. But I am. Stay away from her. And if you don't, expect that retribution will be swift."

"I could have you killed now." But he could see that he'd struck a chord with Hargreave.

"You know it's strange. I've already called the police. They're outside. If something were to happen to me... Well, that would be inconvenient. They know that I'm here."

"Such a powerful man you have to call the cops?"

"Such a powerful man I have contacts everywhere. And I'll use them. Don't forget it."

He turned and walked out of the office, and he didn't look back over his shoulder, for no matter that the other man was issuing threats, he refused to let him put him on the back foot. He refused.

Then he walked out into the sun and smiled. This was back in hand.

Nothing was ever going to change his past.

But today he'd been a different man. Today he hadn't been the playboy. He had done the right thing, and it was a novel enough concept to make him feel.

And now. He had a wedding to plan.

CHAPTER TEN

"SHOPPING FOR wedding dresses is supposed to be fun," said Jessie, pacing the length of the room in the estate.

"It will be," said Maren.

"It will not be. I'm round as an egg. And it's going to be impossible to figure out exactly what size to get. Even though the wedding is in just two weeks."

Two weeks. Already, the headlines had exploded. Already, they were under so much scrutiny, and it had been one day. So technically, she had thirteen days until the wedding.

And he'd said that they would shop for wedding dresses. She wondered if there were any down in the village near here. She could hardly imagine it.

He was intent on making a spectacle, and she wasn't entirely sure what that meant yet.

And that was the thing about him. He came and went as he pleased.

He had been in London on business, so he said.

And when she saw the sleek jet landing just over the rise, she thought about the butterflies in her stomach.

She had no reason to be filled with butterflies. Not at all.

They were doing this to protect their baby.

When he appeared in the estate moments later, she did her best to look bored. She experienced a mountain of messy, horrible feelings whenever she thought of him and it was killing her slowly. By inches.

She couldn't find that neat visual marker she'd counted on for so long.

She tried to imagine a ribbon with his name on it, tied to her feelings, so she could cut it ruthlessly in her mind.

But it was red.

And it just made her angry.

"So are we going down to the village or what?"

"We aren't going to the village." He looked borderline scandalized. "We're going to Paris."

"Paris?"

"Where else?"

That was how she found herself ensconced in the private jet. She hadn't ridden in it yet. She'd never been in a private plane.

It was… It was a stark reminder of just how far apart their positions were.

She had an estate that she owned free and clear and that was a big boon.

She had a couple of million dollars in the bank. Another boon.

But this man was a billionaire. And he controlled more wealth than she would ever be able to fully comprehend. Well, this much wealth.

Butter-soft leather couches on a private jet wealth.

Bedroom on a plane wealth.

Lobster on a plane.

"This is almost outrageously fancy," she said.

He leaned back, his hands behind his head. "When did you miss the memo that I am outrageously fancy?"

She stared at him. Then leaned in and stared harder. He leaned back slightly and that satisfied her.

He was just so ridiculous. As if she hadn't seen him intense.

As if she hadn't seen him as he really was.

Good girl.

The memory of that kept her up at night. It made her sweaty.

Which was not sexy but it was true.

And whatever with that. She saw him. That was the truth of it.

It was, perhaps, the most real reason he'd run.

And that he'd seen her was the biggest reason she'd sent him away.

"I get that that's your facade. Or whatever. It doesn't exactly match up with what I've seen of you, though. You like to play the fool. But I knew the minute I sat down across from you at that poker game that you weren't a fool. I knew the first time I saw you in the casino. Your eyes are too intelligent."

"I'm amazed to hear that you think anyone is intelligent. Given what I know about your gifts."

She shrugged. "It's not a gift. It's a tool. And it isn't intelligence. Just the way my brain is wired. I don't take any particular pride in it, though I have used it, and will continue to use it. I'll be able to remember every stage of our child's development with perfect ease. You know, I wonder about… I have heard so much about the way nostalgia turns memories hazy. I wonder sometimes what that would be like. To let things grow soft so that you can gain a different perspective on them. I never can. I only ever have the perspective I had at the moment. Because I remember everything I saw at that moment. Everything I felt. It robs you of something, I think. Though there are many things that you gain on top of it. I'm not complaining. But I do think that it wouldn't… It's not beneficial for me to be too full of myself about all that. It just isn't."

"That's an interesting perspective. I never thought of it. But I will tell you the memories of my childhood have never grown gauzy. I have never been infused with nostalgia. What was confusing to me as a child is confusing as an adult.

And even if I've tried to sort out what it all means now, I find that I'm unable to."

"Well. That's disappointing. I sort of liked imagining that there were people out there who had it together."

"I have certain things together, that's for certain. And there is something blessed in allowing anonymous evenings to turn into a blur. But our night together never has."

"I suppose I shouldn't be pleased about that," she said.

"You can be pleased about it if you want."

"Then I will be pleased about it. And I will remember that you told me I could be pleased about it for the rest of my life." She didn't bother to hold back the small smile that tugged at the corner of her mouth. "But don't feel too excited about that. After all, I can't forget anything."

"Yes, of course. I promise not to let it go to my head."

"Why Paris?"

A flutter of excitement began to take off in her stomach and it made her feel more than she would like. She had never been to Paris. There had never been a reason to go.

She had spent most of her childhood in the United States until her father moved them to London. Likely running from the law.

But they had never gotten out to see the world. She had traveled since then. She and her sister, running their cons, but it had been to specific places where gambling was a feature. And for the most part, that wasn't major metropolitan areas. Not mainstream ones anyway.

She'd been to Las Vegas more times than she could count. But never Paris.

And she ached with the knowledge that she would go now. With him.

She shut that off. She enjoyed the meal that was served on the plane, and then she went and reclined on the bed for a while, just because she could. When they landed at the airport, they were swept immediately into a luxury car that drove them through the beautiful streets. The architecture was glorious. All stone scrollwork and famous glories. The Eiffel Tower. The Arc de Triomphe. She committed everything to memory. Every detail. She wanted to remember this. Forever. She loved it. She realized that she had her face and palms pressed to the glass on the window. And she felt mildly embarrassed. But not enough to stop. Because these would be her memories. Her chosen memories of this moment.

Paris and all its glory.

"Is it everything you hoped?"

She shot him a shady side eye. "How do you know I've never been here before?"

"You look far too eager for someone who remembers everything. And anyway, you look as if you're trying to save this forever."

"Maybe I am."

"You don't need to be prickly about it."

"Why do you care? What I like, what I'm interested in…"

"It seems like I should know something about the woman who is having my baby."

"Based on what? What do you or I know about functional families?"

"No. On something. Though I can't say what. Movies I've seen or maybe Jiminy Cricket. Isn't that what your conscience is supposed to be shaped like?"

She couldn't help herself. She laughed. "All right. As long as a cricket told you to ask about me, then I allow it."

"Good. Tell me about your mother."

That brought a cascade of images. Her mother laughing, tossing her silky hair over her shoulder. She could remember every time she'd seen her mother do that. Down to the very last time. The time she had left then never come back.

"She was beautiful. Is beautiful, I suppose." As if she had never looked up her mother's picture. She was a socialite who very much enjoyed her visibility.

Jessie was always amazed that her father had let his wife go like that. But she supposed it had to do with starting over in England. Making his new life there. Why bring an American socialite who would offer him nothing in terms of social cachet? Never mind that she was the mother of his children.

But she'd walked out before that anyway. "She was not very interested in being a mother. She was very good at styling hair and letting us try on her gowns. I will give her credit for that. She wasn't protective of them. She treated designer pieces like they might as well be our dress-up clothes. She enjoyed that part of having daughters, I think. She let us use her makeup. She let us play dress-up exhaustively in her bedroom. But then she had her own life to see to. And I can't blame her. Except she left. And I kind of do blame her for that. Which isn't fair because I also left."

"But she left you," he said.

"My father would never have allowed her to take Maren and me. We were too important to him. Too valuable. When we were fourteen and fifteen, he was already using us to crack codes for him and remember things. To run cons. We were better than a computer, he said.

"No. He would never let her walk away with us. She was beautiful. But that was all. She wasn't a real asset to him. It would've put her in danger to bring us, and she never would've been able to start over. Though I think it might be easier for me to forgive her if I truly believed that she missed me."

She felt a slight crack in her heart. It had been

there for years. It was just that now she'd become aware of it.

She did her best not to let it show on her face.

"He taught us to be very analytical. Because our brains do hold so much information. And to access it rather than be bombarded by it you have to learn to use it a very specific way."

"You mentioned files."

"Yes. I keep my important thoughts in files. I can walk through the room that's filled with file cabinets and I can go through them alphabetically. That allows me to put them away so that I'm not assaulted by them when I don't want them, and it allows me to come up with a system to help me go through the vast amount of knowledge I have. The other thing he taught us to do was read body language. And manipulate people based on who we assess that they are."

"There's a term for that, isn't there?"

"Yes. A mentalist. I suppose that's what I am. I'm sure there must be some very good things that could be done with the skill set, but I was never shown them. It has helped me, though. To insulate me. Protect me from being swallowed up by my emotions. I learned early on what was important."

"Protecting yourself."

"Yes."

"That's how life is when the adults around

you don't protect you," he said, his tone far too knowing.

"Yes."

"But we are protecting our baby. He or she will never have to wonder. And he will not have to build up those defenses."

"But she might need them," said Jessie. "Imagine if she has a brain like mine. I hope she doesn't. I hope she's desperately normal. And I'll think she's exceptional all the same. All mothers do, don't they?" She laughed. "How quickly I forgot my own story. My mother didn't think I was exceptional."

"And you were. Objectively. And so I think the conclusion to be drawn here is that when a mother does not find her child exceptional it is not a commentary on whether or not the child is. It is simply a commentary on the mother."

"Maybe. What about your mother?"

He cleared his throat. "She thought I was exceptional. She loved me. More than anything. She told me all the time she never understood what her life was about, who she was or what the day-to-day meant until she had me. When she was alive, I was happy. But I didn't realize just how much she held everything together. I didn't realize just how much she was protecting me. Because once she was gone, I was no longer under the illusion that my father felt similarly."

"I'm sorry... What happened?"

"We don't need to speak of it."

And she realized that he couldn't speak of it.

"Okay."

For the first time in her recent memory, she was comfortable letting something go. She wasn't certain why; it was just she knew she didn't want to hurt him. She cared about him.

It was such a dangerous thing because when he had left her days ago, she had felt so bereft. Even though she had asked for it. She wasn't reliable when it came to him. Not in any way.

She had made one mistake after another with him. And she was used to being unerring. Analytical. She had never been analytical with him, not for one moment of their association. And she continued not to be. Her own mind made no sense around him.

Her mind was playing tricks on her, and that was part of why she had grown up so analytical. To make it so the mind as strong as hers could never do that.

She turned to face him, looked at his strong profile. Those beautiful eyes...

And it was all feeling when she looked at him. Nothing to do with analysis or equations. She couldn't even tell what he was thinking.

She realized that with alacrity. When she had first met him she felt like she could read him, and now the more she got entangled with him the less she felt like she could.

It just felt like…

Feeling. It was all she could think to call it.

"Are we nearly to our shopping destination?"

"Yes. There will be people there, waiting to take a picture. I called ahead. The best paparazzi photos are staged."

"Really?"

"Of course. If you ever see a photograph with favorable lighting that immediately tells you what brands the woman in the picture is wearing, you can be certain that she called the photographers out to the scene herself."

"That is brilliant."

"You're a con artist. That never occurred to you?"

"Shocking though you may find it, I have not often spent my time ruminating on celebrity. I had bigger fish to fry."

"Well, fry your little fish out of the car," he said as they pulled up to the curb. "And smile."

CHAPTER ELEVEN

HE WATCHED AS Jessie got out of the car and posed like an absolute champion for the photographer that was waiting.

She caught on quickly, and she understood the need for all of this.

He got out of the car and followed behind, doing his own best to look irritated by the proceedings. He put a protective hand on her, another hand on her stomach. Each moment that he spent touching her was like pressing his palm against a naked flame.

This woman. Would he ever get used to the proximity of her? She was asking all kinds of questions he didn't easily have answers to. Well, he could have easily answered how his mother had died, except the words often got stuck in his throat, and he didn't want to speak of his dead brother. More than anything he did not wish to speak of that.

But also, she was asking how he knew what a child needed. And perhaps the answer was in the deficits. He leaned in and whispered in her ear as they walked into the door of the boutique where he had made a private appointment for them. "I think I know what our child needs because I know what we didn't get."

She turned to look up at him, eyes wide, her lips parted slightly. And he knew that would make a fantastic photo.

As soon as they were inside, they had privacy.

"It's more believable if we keep this entirely private."

"Right."

But he stopped talking about believability because the designer and a seamstress came into the foyer of the store and greeted them.

"Miss Lockwood," the woman said—they had agreed to use Jessie's alias while they traveled, because why court trouble? "Very good to have you here. We have pulled aside some of our most popular and accommodating designs."

Jessie laughed. "I assume you mean to accommodate my stomach."

"The baby," the woman said, smiling, tapping Jessie's bump, which caused Jessie to look up at him in irritation.

He shrugged.

He followed Jessie and the two women back into the dressing room. Where she was summarily divested of her clothing, without even being ushered behind the curtain.

"Isn't that..." He couldn't help but lean forward in interest when Jessie's bra was removed. "Dressing room?"

"No need," he said. "Nothing I haven't seen."

She opened her mouth like a fish, opened and closed, opened and closed. But then said nothing.

He had a feeling he would get an earful about that later. But he didn't mind getting an earful from her.

As he sat there watching as she was wrapped in gown after gown, he realized something very strange.

He had lived a very lonely life. He couldn't recall having a relationship that was long or strong enough with someone else to be able to anticipate what they would do in response to something. But with Jessie, he could already imagine it.

She would lecture him, on her modesty. And maybe then afterward she would tease him. Like she had done coming out of her bath the other day. She had dropped that towel and showed him the whole of her beautiful backside before dressing herself. She wasn't shy, and even if she were, it was clear that her desire to one-up him outweighed any kind of modesty she might possess.

She knew that he responded too eagerly to her body to ever remain completely cool and collected when she was nude, and she was happy to dress up, in that red dress as she had done that day that he had come to find out about the pregnancy, and again that day when she had dropped her towel.

He had a feeling it wouldn't take her long to figure out how to use this to her advantage.

He was excited then, not because he was getting a good view of her body, though that, too, but mostly because he knew that about her.

He *knew* her.

At least in some capacity. And it was a strange and unique feeling that he didn't want to let go of.

She tried on many flowing gowns, with the last one being more fitted, showing off the swell of her stomach, and there was an elemental need that fired through his veins that he had no control over. He stood. "That one."

"The lady gets to choose her own gown," the designer said, sniffing.

"I am paying for the lady's gown, and I like her in this one. I want to see her body. I want to see her curves."

"Just for that, I think I might agitate for one of the others," she said, but he could see by the way she looked at herself in the mirror that she liked this one best, too. It annoyed her she agreed with him. He was amused by that realization.

"She'll take this one."

She bought shoes and a veil, and by the time they swept back out onto the Paris streets, their packages safely ensconced in their town car, she was glaring at him.

"We're walking just down this way to go and get some dinner. I've made us a reservation."

He sensed her soften beside him. The mention of food might be enough to tame her.

"Oh."

"I thought you might enjoy a nice meal."

"No. You thought there might be some nice pictures from the nice meal."

"I can think both."

"You are just as much of a con artist as I am. You said that. But I don't think I fully realized it until now. You're always operating on multiple frequencies. That's what you have to do."

He nodded. "That is what you have to do. At least, it's what I've had to do all of my life."

She fell into step beside him. "You're not a playboy, are you?"

"Oh, I am."

"I didn't mean it in the way that… I mean, I'm certain you're a slut."

He barked a laugh. "What?"

"Yes. You have a reputation for sleeping with anything that moves."

"Not anything."

"Okay," she relented. "Not anything. But the overriding opinion is that you are free and easy with your favors."

"I am. And you aren't."

"Out of necessity."

"Understood."

"But I mean you aren't shallow. Or an idiot. That's a game that you like to play because it lets you be in control. People underestimate you. I get that. That's what I do with my looks. I go out of my way to get written off as a bimbo. It's funny. You know my sister seduced so many men without ever letting them touch her. She flattered them. Appealed to them. And she could get them to give her so many things without actually giving them anything. It is amazing what people do when they think you are stupid and they can show you something. It's amazing what you can get from them." She frowned. "I hate that. I hate that I know that. I hate that I think that way. I think maybe I'm not a con artist, and yet I have been forced to live as one. I like gambling. I like winning, and it has taken me until this moment to really…" She trailed off, suddenly looking worried.

"What?"

"Do you ever worry that you're wicked?"

He thought of his father. Who had been difficult always, but had gone into some sort of darkness that terrified Ewan mostly because… he recognized it. "Yes. I do."

"Me, too. All the time. How can you not worry when you're so like…? When you're so like him?"

She was talking about herself, and he knew that. Yet, he shared that feeling. It resonated throughout his entire body.

Because yes. He knew that. He knew it well. "That's when you dedicate your life to revenge," he said, his tone dry.

She laughed. "Oh, I don't have the energy for that. I want to have a life. That's what I was trying to do."

They arrived at the restaurant, and he could see more people taking their pictures, just as he'd anticipated. He overrode the doorman and opened the door for Jessie himself, ushering her inside with a protective arm. They were then led to a table in an alcove. It was a small restaurant with only ten tables, but they were right by the window so that they could be photographed.

"And what exactly have you decided to dedicate your life to?" he asked when they were seated and assured the waiter that they would be taking the prix fixe menu.

With no alcohol for the lady.

"To being happy. At least, that was my plan."

"Win enough money to be settled."

"Yes. When I won the estate, I was…overwhelmed. Overcome. I couldn't believe I'd done it. I'd set myself up for life. And given myself a home. There was never a moment when my father's house felt like a home, no matter where it was. I was always so aware that it was simply his domain. The place where he and other criminals hatched schemes and took advantage of people.

It never felt safe. Even being part of his circle. Or maybe being part of it most of all."

"You were part of it. You're not so different from me. Your father made decisions for you. About how comfortable you would be. About how you would spend your time. You are nothing more than a thing to him." He twirled his wineglass on the table. "I spoke to your father."

Her eyes went round. "You what?"

"I decided to go and introduce myself to him. Since I am going to be his son-in-law, after all."

"He's a dangerous man. I thought the entire point of this was to avoid him."

"No, the entire point of this is to get rid of him once and for all. I'm not a man who lets other people determine how I behave. Your father needed to understand the power balance."

"He's dangerous."

"So he told me. Repeatedly. Men who are so dangerous don't need to tell you. Anyone who has any substance whatsoever will simply show you. He's violent, that's clear. But he is not half as clever as he thinks he is, and that is going to be the end of him."

She looked away. "He doesn't forget, though."

He reached out and cupped her chin, forced her to meet his gaze. "Perhaps not. He remembers everything, just like you, but I think that because of that he often does not see. Often does not understand. That some are smart in other ways, and who might have stronger motivation than he realizes." He let that sit with her for a moment. "He's a sociopath, isn't he?"

Her eyes widened a fraction. "Yes. I suppose that's a fair characterization."

"And you aren't."

"How do you know that?" She suddenly looked worried. "I mean really, how do you know that? Because I worry sometimes. I was just saying to you I don't like conning people, and I think that's true. But sometimes… When I won that poker game against you, I felt like I was high. I might as well have taken an illegal substance. I was so thrilled with myself. And I knew at that moment that it was a little bit sad that I was finished with my games because my games made me feel alive."

"You're not a sociopath, because you worry that you might be. Do you think your father has ever given one moment's thought to whether or not he was hurting the people around him? Do you think he just does what is expedient for him?"

"You're right."

"My father wasn't a sociopath. In many ways, that's worse. He was often in a cycle of shame and regret but then his rages were unparalleled. His lows were more than the entire sea."

"I'm sorry," she said. "It sounds horrible. But your mother…"

"We can be done with this."

Dinner was served after, and it was delicious, but he could not keep his mind on the meal before him when he was consumed with Jessie.

"Dinner was delicious," she said when they finished. They walked back out onto the street. He couldn't escape the feeling that he should be touching her. And yet, he couldn't bring himself to close the distance between them.

"The hotel we're staying in is just down there."

"Okay," she said.

"Do you wish to know about my mother?"

He kept that space of air between them, made sure that he wasn't touching her at all.

"It seems like the thing you want to tell me least."

"That isn't an answer."

She stopped and looked at him. "I don't want to hurt for you. But I do. I already do. You make me act so out of character. You make me... From the moment that I met you, and I mean, saw you, not met you, I have thought of nothing else. I was obsessed with you. And that has never happened to me before. I'm focused. I've had to be. But you have disrupted everything. You wrecked everything. Look at this. Look at me," she said, gesturing to her stomach. "You have changed me forever more, and there has never and will never be anything the way that it was. I can never have that uncomplicated and free life, because of you. *Because of you.* I'm not even sure that I want it. Because it feels good to change. But I'm afraid. I'm afraid of hurting even more for you. Feeling even more for you. I'm already carrying your baby. I don't want to crack myself open. Not again. But also, I have a feeling that this is the one thing that you need to tell me. Really."

"Is that a yes?"

"Yes."

He nodded and turned away, continuing to walk down the street. "When I was eleven years old, she died giving birth."

It was a surprisingly easy thing to say. Such a surprisingly simple thing. No real explanation was required, and he was shocked when that story fell out of his mouth. So complete, with so few words.

"Oh," she said. Not a simple sound, but one as if she had been punched in the stomach.

"I saw it. Her. And the baby."

"I'm sorry…"

"There's no need to be sorry."

Her eyes filled with tears. "I'm sorry." She said it as if she was full of wonder. The strangest tone.

"I just… It's terribly sad."

"Yes, it is. But there's nothing you can do about those sorts of tragedies. They just are. If you're lucky they don't turn you into a monster. My father wasn't so lucky."

"Did it happen at…the estate?"

He nodded.

"That's why you don't like being there. You don't. I can feel it."

"No. I don't like being there. But it's less about that and more about what happened right after, and years that followed. He beat me after she died, to stop me from crying."

"Ewan…" She breathed the word, a note of shocked horror.

"He would have his heir be perfect. And then there was all the time after. All the time that I spent being abused and locked away by my father. All the rage that I felt, all of it swamps me when I go back there."

"That's terrible. It's an amazing thing that there are so many different kinds of terrible in the world. I've only lived one of them. My life has been so sheltered and small that I've only ever really put thought into my sort of terrible. Maybe that's why I worried I was a sociopath. Well, that and my father. You do worry that that sort of thing is hereditary."

"You love your sister."

She nodded. "I do. And Maren… She's soft. And all I ever wanted was to protect her softness because it's so beautiful and lovely in this ugly, ugly world."

"But what about you?" he asked. "Who protected you?"

"Maren tries. You've seen it."

"But you saw things, didn't you?" he asked, his voice heavy.

She nodded. "When Maren and I were girls we were sometimes used as decoys. Once I pretended to be lost in a train station, specifically to catch the attention of an elderly man. He comforted me, and he told me about his granddaughter. I told my father his granddaughter was his weakness."

"How old were you?"

He could see remorse rising in her like a tide; he could see it in her eyes. "Nine. But it didn't matter. My father kidnapped the man's granddaughter. They hurt her. I could hear her screaming. The man told my father he'd give him anything he wanted…anything at all."

"And then what?"

"That night I helped them both escape. I knew exactly how to get them out of the compound. I knew every code. But I will never get the sound of screams out of my head. I will never be able to make that moment any less clear."

"Did your father find out you did it?"

She smiled. "Of course he did. I made sure he knew Maren had nothing to do with it. I accepted his beating and I considered it a trade. He would have killed that girl. But I realized that I couldn't walk through life feeling so much. I couldn't have emotion attached to every image, or I'd never have a sleep that wasn't made of nightmares. So

I cut them off. I worried maybe I would never be able to get my feelings back. But…" A tear slid down her cheek. "I met you and felt something. We made love and I felt something. You told me that story and I feel something. This story is very sad indeed."

He looked at her and he felt…indescribably desolate for having caused her tears. This was perhaps the best reason of all to continue to be the playboy. That man felt so little he could never have such hollowed-out feelings over his mother and dead brother.

He could never feel like killing Jessie's father with his bare hands.

Or offering comfort to Jessie, like he wanted to do now.

Even though he wasn't certain how to do it.

"You went to see my father?"

"Yes. I'm not afraid of him. I don't feel fear for myself. I was broken of that when I was a boy. Because there were a few times when I was certain I was going to die. I knew what dying looked like. When you go through those things as a child, I think you become dead to them later on. I don't worry for my own life."

They continued walking until they reached the hotel, which was glorious naturally, but mostly, he just saw her.

"Our room awaits," he said.

They went through the lobby—all sleek black

marble and highly polished gold. He realized then that he could have her if he wished. Because she looked soft and sympathetic to him. And their bodies already knew what to do when they were alone. They already gave in to such things. They had already built a pattern of falling into each other's arms because it felt right. Because it felt necessary. Because it would erase the pain that he felt over having bared his soul to her in regard to his mother.

And he needed to avoid it. He needed to tell himself no. Because he had to prove that he had control here. He had given in to her because it was easy. Because he had let himself believe for a moment that he was the playboy that he pretended to be.

He'd been so dead inside when his father had died that he'd told himself there was nothing left in himself that felt.

And then, when he had come to her the day he learned about the baby, when he had run…

He had run away.

Like the frightened boy he'd been. A boy who hadn't been able to run. Who hadn't been able to escape the estate. And it was as if he had fled on behalf of that child.

But he would not fall into a lack of control now. He would not give himself over to this thing between them. Because he had agreed to come back. He had known he needed to care for her.

To marry her. To make his child legitimate, whether he felt that mattered or not. He would give his child everything.

And then, in the end, he and Jessie would live their own lives. Separately.

Because she needed him now. The child needed him now. But they would not always.

Tonight he would not touch her.

Tonight he would be…different. Not the playboy, but not himself, either. Something better.

When the elevator reached the penthouse, he let her get off first. It was a mirror of that night they had spent together. And he would not allow it to end the same way.

"Go and get your rest. You must be tired."

She looked at him, somewhat shocked. "Yes. Of course. That's… It's a good idea. I will get some rest."

"We can do some sightseeing tomorrow if you like. And then we will go back to Scotland."

"Sightseeing and everything. For a whole day. You know how to show a girl a good time."

"We could go straight back."

She fixed him with a pout that was far more charming than it had the right to be. "Don't be mean. You promised to show me Paris."

"I suppose I have."

CHAPTER TWELVE

JESSIE FELT ODDLY DEFLATED having been sent to bed by herself, but she knew that it was a good thing.

She knew that it was better for her to learn to spend some time with him without…

Well, too bad for her in the way her brain worked; all she did was think about him naked, and picture him in excruciating detail whenever he came to mind.

So maybe that was the thing. She needed to build some new images around Ewan.

It was so difficult. Because she liked the naked ones.

But he had promised to take her out and about in the city today. So she supposed she needed to act happy. And grateful.

She paused, putting her outfit on for the day. Just a black stretchy dress that covered her baby bump, and a pair of boots that were also black. She looked a bit witchy, and she liked it.

She was using him. She was using him the way that she had always used people.

The way her father had taught her to.

And now that she felt things—more and more things—it made her ache.

She hadn't meant to. She'd wanted so badly to get away from it. To get away from using.

She wanted her own life that she could have on her own terms. She didn't want to use anybody. She really didn't.

But she didn't know another way to be either.

That made her feel indescribably sad.

Did that make her a better person because she felt sad at the thought?

How did you ever know if you were or weren't using someone? She had used him that first night to lose her virginity. To experience pleasure. She had used him that second time for the same reason, but also to try and stop her heart from bleeding out, to do something to make her feel like she could hang on to a memory of him. And now she was using him to keep her safe. Using his money, using his power and influence.

Did people only ever use each other? Were they all like her father, just on different sides of the law? Did they use people with varying degrees of selfishness?

She had no idea how she was supposed to know.

This was why she didn't feel. Or why she

hadn't historically. Because with feeling came worry. Trauma. Guilt.

She loved her sister. But the truth was, Maren was very easy to love. And Jessie had known her all of her life.

Maybe if she hadn't, she would simply use Maren, too.

Or maybe she did. Because she needed Maren to tell her whether or not she was being a good person, and to set boundaries and parameters for her. Maybe she used Maren as her external conscience. Her cricket.

She did love her, though. She was certain of that. She really was certain of that.

She put some red lipstick on and decided that she looked like a very Parisian witch, so there was that.

Then she met him out in the living area. She had not been prepared for him. She never could be. He was wearing a white shirt, the sleeves rolled up to his elbows, showing his spectacular forearms.

He had the most beautiful hands she'd ever seen. And she could remember every pair of hands she'd ever seen if she tried hard enough.

"Good morning," she said.

"Good morning," he said.

He gestured to the table. "I had an array of baked goods brought for you. I thought we might want to eat before we go get to the sightseeing."

"So," she said. "Is this primarily to make more splash in the press, to make my father feel like he can't make any moves toward me?"

"Yes," he said.

"And here I thought you just liked me."

He looked at her, his gaze cool and assessing. "You know you have a gold fleck in your right eye?" she asked.

"What kind of question is that?"

"It's an observation and a question. But I noticed that your eyes were different the first time we met. And I wondered if you had ever noticed."

"I don't spend that much time staring at my own face."

"You should. It's a decent face," she said.

His expression was cool, but she could see amusement in his eyes. "Thank you for that."

She inclined her head. "Of course."

"And don't take it personally, Jessie. I don't like anyone."

She frowned. "Do you think you'll like the baby?" It would be difficult if he didn't. But then, would she like the baby? She had no experience with babies. It was a concern.

"Do most people like their own children?"

"I don't know. There are certainly TV shows that suggest some people like their children. And in fact, choose to spend time with their families. I guess I choose to spend quite a lot of time with my sister. But we never really had a choice. And soon she's going to be a princess and move into a castle."

"I don't really understand that."

"She won a castle. She just can't move in until Christmas."

"Well, all right, then. But what exactly is your point?"

"I'm not sure if I would've chosen to spend that much time with her if I didn't have to. So I guess I'm saying I don't have empirical evidence that people like their families."

"Did you want to go sightseeing or not?"

She nodded vigorously. "I very much do."

"Then let's go."

"It's okay that you're using this to get to my father," she said once they were in the car headed somewhere she didn't know.

"Thank you. I'm glad to have your approval."

"I was just thinking that we all always use each other. It can't be helped. You're only with people when you need things from them."

"I can't say that I ever thought about it."

"I think about it a lot. My whole childhood was so isolated. It isn't like we went to school."

"Never?"

"You did?"

"Yes. A boarding school. But still. I was with other children my age." He looked away from her. "I had friends."

"How nice. That you did get a reprieve from

being around your father." She meant it. She wished she'd had a reprieve from hers, but she didn't resent him.

"Yes. School was my only real escape. This persona was very effective there. People like the one who's always quick with a laugh or a sarcastic comment. I found that it could obscure the reality of things. I made myself who I am because of that school."

"I think I never had the chance to develop a *persona*." What she'd done with her feelings wasn't about showing a particular thing to others; it was about protecting herself. "I've been many different people. It all just feels more like a mask that I take on and off at the end of the day. It would be nice to have a persona. It feels a little bit more stable."

"So you were kept at home. How did you get an education?"

She laughed. She couldn't help herself. "I remember everything. Everything. So if I read a mathematical formula, I remember how to implement it. Also, that kind of thing just makes sense in my head."

"Right. You're a genius."

"I suppose. Though I think it's more of a very helpful party trick. Regardless, the education part wasn't the issue."

"You didn't have friends."

She shook her head. "Only my sister. Who at

least understood me, but the problem with that is… When someone understands you so well you don't have to learn to be understood. You don't have to learn to connect. We just think the same. I don't know how to make another person understand me."

"I think most people don't know that. And it's what causes a lot of the great strife in the world."

"Humans are needlessly complicated," she said.

"On that, we can agree."

They ended up walking along the river and stopping at various market stalls.

He bought her lunch at a café, and then they continued to walk until they got to the Musée d'Orsay.

"I could take you to the Louvre, but I confess that I prefer this one."

"Why is that?"

"It's more than expected."

"I just think you're a hipster," she said.

And much to her surprise, he laughed. "That's a new one. I've never been accused of that before."

"Have you ever known anyone well enough to have them accuse you of anything?"

He looked at her for a long moment. "No."

Her delight in everything was infectious.

She was odd. And he hadn't noticed how much

that was true when she had been playing the part of the seductress the night she had won the poker game. When she was angry, her quirks were also not as apparent.

But he was peeling back the layers on her, and he could see that it was true. She didn't have experience getting to know someone. Not outside of a con.

It was something they had in common. Because he wasn't certain when he'd last gotten to know someone, either.

She had appreciated everything, but when they walked into the museum, everything was different. She looked around; her jaw dropped as they walked through the first wing, filled with statuary. Then they made their way through various art exhibits, and she took everything in, and he wondered what it would be like to remember every detail. Of such beauty.

There was a van Gogh display in a black room where your senses were cut off from everything but the gloriously detailed artwork.

And when Jessie stood in front of *Starry Night*, her hands clasped tightly and pressed against her chest, he watched as tears formed at the corners of her eyes and slid down her cheeks.

"Are you all right?"

"Yes," she said. "It's just… I've seen this painting. It isn't the same. It isn't the same as seeing it in person. And I will remember every detail of this forever. And what a gift. To be given such a beautiful memory."

Memories.

The most valuable gift that can ever be given to her, because they were indelible.

His chest felt like it had been split with a large ax. Because he had never given to anyone before.

Revenge was a selfish pursuit. He had been consumed in his own need to harm his father for so many years that he… He had not made connections.

He had lost touch with those friends from school as he had made himself into a crasser version of himself as the years went on and he'd perfected his facade.

But this was real. The joy on her face. The way that she looked at him.

There was no artifice here. No revenge, no con. Just connection.

And it did something to him. Shifted something inside him. Changed him. Utterly. Absolutely.

He didn't know if he was intrigued or if he wanted to turn away. He'd wanted to find something other than the facade he'd cultivated. He wanted something other than the ash that was left in his mouth after his father died. The bitterness of revenge gone satisfied, and cold.

She'd shown him he could feel something.

He could not deny this moment. The look of

pure ecstasy on her face as she took in every brushstroke of the artwork in front of her.

He vowed then to give her more memories. There were so many gifts that could be given away. Thrown away. Forgotten about.

The memory would stay with Jessie forever, and he realized that made his every interaction with her so much more perilous. So much more precious.

She was a rare thing. And she had been abused all of her life.

He felt the sudden urge to shield her entirely. From anything unpleasant in the world.

She stayed at the museum for hours. Until it was dark outside.

And he had never fancied himself a great lover of museums, but watching her was something that he might never tire of.

What a strange thing. To care for someone like that.

The thought brought him up short.

Caring for her.

And she was at risk.

He thought of her father again.

He would kill that man himself before he ever…

And there it was. His father's violence making itself known, crowding into this moment when he had felt human.

He hated that. Hated his old man with a burning passion.

It had become everything he was, and yet…

He had not changed a thing.

He was having a child. He had not ended the bloodline.

His father was dead, and his mother was still gone.

Nothing was fixed.

When they finally finished and went back to the penthouse, he left her again, without touching her. Because he needed to distance himself from these feelings.

He couldn't afford to have them.

He couldn't afford to have any.

CHAPTER THIRTEEN

JESSIE WAS STILL lost in the beauty of their trip to Paris when the day of the wedding came.

Maren was fussing about, and arranging her skirt, fiddling with her flowers.

"This really should be you," said Jessie, looking at her sister.

"Why?" Maren asked.

"Because you're a romantic. And I never have been."

Maren laughed. "I think you probably are a secret romantic."

"Why do you think that?"

"The dress that you chose is the definition of a princess wedding gown."

"It is the definition of a dress that wasn't going to get too tight for me in a couple of weeks between when I bought it and today."

"Sure."

The annoying thing was her sister was right. It was difficult not to feel romantic.

They were getting married in a beautiful chapel down in the village, and she happened to know for a fact that the entire thing had been decorated with white lights and manzanita bows that made the entire thing look like something out of *A Midsummer Night's Dream*.

She would've said that she did not believe in the romance of weddings, or fairies, but being in Scotland with Ewan made her feel slightly different.

He hadn't touched her, though.

In the two weeks since he had returned, he had not touched her.

He had taken her to Paris, they had bought a dress. He had taken her to the Musée d'Orsay and he had shown her something so beautiful she did not think that she would ever recover from it. And he had not touched her.

She didn't understand why. He didn't want her anymore. She was getting fairly round with the baby, and it was entirely possible he wasn't attracted to the shape of a pregnant body.

That made her feel sad, but she supposed it was understandable. People had the taste that they had, after all.

As if she hadn't made all kinds of proclamations when she had said she would marry him. About not wanting things to be physical. She had to. But it felt like things were shifting between them.

Why do you think that?

She stood there and stared at her reflection in the mirror. The woman there was unrecognizable. She had her natural hair color. Something she saw so rarely that it just didn't feel like hers.

She was wearing a wedding gown. She was pregnant. She had makeup on that was designed to highlight her features, not shift them into something else.

She was Jessie. She supposed.

And she had never really been all that familiar with Jessie.

By cutting her emotions off, she'd cut herself off with it.

She'd done it to be safe. He'd challenged that, and at first, she'd been afraid of it. At first, she'd gone back and forth, wanting it but fearing it all the same.

But then she'd seen him. And he'd seen her.

And somehow it was helping her see herself anew.

She walked up to the mirror without thinking and touched it, her finger pressed against the reflection of her own hand.

"Are you okay?" Maren asked.

She jumped and took a step backward. "Yes. I'm fine. We should probably head to the church."

"Probably," Maren agreed.

It was going to be a huge and highly publicized event because in the time since they had announced their engagement, the headlines all over the world had exploded. There was going to be a made-for-TV movie about their romance. Well, not their romance, but one just like it. About a man who loses his estate in a poker game, and then falls madly in love with the woman who won it.

A great story, she thought. But not…theirs.

But it was having the effect that he'd wanted it to. If anyone made a move toward her, it would be so highly publicized, so apparent, that nobody would ever be able to walk away from it without a life of imprisonment.

She was no longer an asset to her father that outweighed the liability of acquiring her.

And that was the gift.

It really was.

So she supposed it didn't matter if he touched her or not. Her feelings didn't matter.

She didn't even know what her feelings were. But she had them now.

Did he?

She had been drawn to him from the first moment she had seen him. She knew it was the same for him, but would he ever let himself feel it?

They were both broken; he was right about that. But they'd seen each other. Didn't that matter?

It had changed her.

Would it ever change him?

She'd seen hints of it. She knew he wasn't the

man he'd pretended to be for so many years. He was caring, and intense. He was strong and he was...

Ewan. The same way she was just Jessie.

"You look sad," said Maren.

"I guess I'm a little sad. I never dreamed about getting married. I sort of wish I had. So that I could enjoy a part of this."

"Is that really what's bothering you?"

She didn't know what was bothering her. She was trying to figure it out. Her brain was a fantastic and useful computer and it couldn't seem to put the data set together to figure out what exactly was the issue now.

So what good was it to her?

"Come on," said Maren. "You have to get married."

Maren was irrepressibly excited and Jessie had a feeling it was down to her bridesmaid dress being princess-like and frothy.

She allowed herself to feel a small measure of happiness that Maren had gotten through all this with her... Maren-ness intact.

That was, perhaps, the greatest testament to what she'd done in the years they lived with her father. She'd protected Maren. She was still able to be soft and excited.

And you?

Well, she'd committed graver sins.

You saved that girl; how long will you punish yourself for being a pawn?

She wasn't punishing herself; she was protecting herself.

But not now.

No, not now. She couldn't, not with him, and she'd known that from the beginning.

It was why she'd pushed him away, then been angry about it. Because she wanted it, but she'd been afraid of it.

So much of her life was grounded in fear.

The fear of what her father might have made her.

The fear of her own complicity in the things he'd done.

She was tired of being afraid.

Ewan had given her new feelings. Bright feelings. Glorious feelings. She wanted to feel them, and with that there was the possibility she could feel bad things.

But she was Jessie. Wholly. And that made it seem worth it.

The drive to the church seemed to go on forever, and when they got there, she was shocked by the sheer number of people milling about. She was ushered through a side door where she would be concealed from everyone, including Ewan.

She was his pregnant bride. She was surprised how unbothered by that people seemed to be.

They had been given a brief overview of the way the ceremony would work, and after they had been there in a side room for a few moments,

Maren was ushered out the door to walk down the aisle.

She was walking by herself, the only member of the bridal party, but she was obviously the maid of honor.

The most important person in attendance.

And then the music changed and it was time for her.

Of course, her father wasn't giving her away. She was giving herself away.

Because she owned herself. She owned her life.

And she was using…

She stepped to the edge of the sanctuary, all the thoughts dissolved in her head.

Because there he was. Standing at the head of the altar in a black suit jacket and a kilt. The dark green-and-blue tartan was perfect, masculine and went with his eyes, and she wondered if it was a family pattern.

It was hard to say with him because he did resent his father, but also against his will seemed to have some thoughts about bloodlines and succession. He was here, after all.

And he was handsome.

His hair curled around the collar of his suit jacket, just perfectly, pushed back off his forehead, and his eyes were stunning.

She just kept her focus on those eyes as she made her way down the aisle.

Her heart felt sore.

And as she got closer, it only felt like it was getting even more sore, as if it was growing, even.

She took his hand in hers when she reached the front of the room; all eyes were on her, she suddenly realized. It was as if this missing piece had locked into place, and everything suddenly became clear.

She could make sense of what she was thinking because she wasn't thinking.

She was feeling.

And she'd kept wanting to make it all clean and neat.

She'd kept wanting to make it all a con. She wanted to think about who was using whom, and why. She wanted to try and figure out the plan, the aim, the end goal.

And yes, she was using him in some regard to keep her and the baby safe. But mostly, she liked being with him.

Mostly, he was important to her.

Standing in front of him was like standing in front of *Starry Night*.

Every detail on his face, every line, every beautiful element that made him who he was, filled her, consumed her. Made her want to weep.

She couldn't put names to all of this because they were feelings.

She had never been taught to prioritize feelings. She'd been taught to push them down. Put them away.

She had been given the mind that she had be-cause it mattered more than her heart.

And she realized now that wasn't true. Right at that moment, her heart mattered very much, and it was the thing driving all of this.

Her heart was now pounding so hard that she felt dizzy.

She felt for him.

She could feel.

She'd always been able to care. She had just been afraid to. Because much like desire, it would be something she would never be able to forget the finer details of.

And it would be horrible. And wonderful. All at the same time.

And if she lost him, if she lost this, then what would she have?

And she would lose him. Because this was never about forever.

The vows they spoke were traditional, and they made her tremble. Because she'd never had tra-ditional in all of her life, and here she was in a white wedding dress holding hands with the most beautiful man she'd ever seen, saying sa-cred words in front of a priest.

She was pregnant, so there was that. That bit of the nontraditional, which at least made her feel like herself.

And when it was time to kiss, her heart leaped up to her throat, and he reached out and caressed her face, his fingertips moving slowly down her cheek. She searched his eyes for a sign that he wanted to kiss her. For a sign that this was real. For a sign that he felt anything at all, the way that she did.

Because she felt too much. Everything.

And then he leaned in, and it was like the whole world slowed down.

This was different. Different than the first time, which had been driven by uncontrollable lust. And different than the last time, which had been all lust and anger and desperation.

This was different. Because she knew that it was more than sex. Because she knew that it was more than a decision she'd made by thinking.

This was nothing less than her whole heart.

Then he leaned in, his mouth touching hers, and she ignited.

There in a church in front of everybody.

She wrapped her arms around his neck and clung to him, every beat of her heart trying to teach her a new language.

This language of feeling.

It was new and it was terrifying. Wonderful and debilitating.

She felt like she was being set free and shackled all at once, and maybe that was how everyone felt in these sorts of situations, but how would she know? Because she had never known anyone who could tell her.

His kiss was everything she remembered and more. Warm and wonderful and perfect.

And she breathed him in and clung to him, the memory of the vows they had just spoken a promise that echoed through her soul.

And when they parted, everyone in the church clapped for them as the priest announced them as man and wife.

She didn't know any of these people. All these people out in the crowd wishing them well. And she knew that it wasn't real. That it was all based on their feelings for him and his proximity to power. But she couldn't deny that it made her feel something. This moment when it seemed as if she was part of a community of people. Rather than on the outside.

It was also…strange. Now that she had opened herself up to the possibility of feeling, it all seemed muddled. Intense beyond the rational.

But she supposed that was the issue. She had moved beyond rational. She had gone to another place entirely.

She had opened up her heart. And that was the thing she had always been the most afraid of. Because her heart wasn't full of files.

She had all this knowledge in her head, and yet it wasn't any use to her when it came to this. To feelings.

She didn't know what to do with all of this.

She didn't know what to do with herself.

But she was there with him, and they were married. But it was nothing. For nothing except the protection of the baby.

Suddenly, she felt like she couldn't breathe.

But he was there. He looked at her and squeezed her hand, and it was easy for her to believe it was because he felt something, too.

It was easy for her to believe that it was because he was swept up in the same tide of emotion. In the vows they had just spoken as strangers clapped for them.

He wasn't, though; she could see it. In his eyes.

Because she had clear memories of those eyes. And she knew what it was like when they were filled with passion. She knew what it was when they were filled with emotion. Vulnerability, as they had been when he had told her about his mother.

It made her ache. Tremble. She felt as if she was having an episode.

Because it was like a wall had come down within her and suddenly, she was just so aware.

She had been pleased that she was hurt for him that night in Paris, as it had been evidence to her that she wasn't a sociopath.

But it was beyond that now. She wasn't pleased that she had feelings. She simply had them.

It was like all of her self-protection was gone. All of it.

And all she could do was cling to him, the object of this pain, and let him walk her back down the aisle.

She smiled, because she was very good at playing a part, above all things, even when everything inside her was eroding.

They got into the car that was waiting for them, and she began to breathe a little bit better. They would go back to the estate; they would…

She realized they were driving away from the estate.

"Where are we going?"

"To the airport."

"What?"

"We are going on a honeymoon."

"I don't understand. Even if we were doing that we could fly out of the estate."

"Too private. I am ostentatiously taking you on a honeymoon."

Of course he was. Because this was all about the show, and she had to remember that. Before she let her tender heart begin to beat in response to the idea of him taking her on a romantic trip, she reminded herself that this was about showing her father that he cared for her, so that her father would believe that the hammer would fall upon him were he to make a move toward her.

"Oh. But Maren…"

"She knows. And don't worry. She's been secreted off to her very own luxury private chalet where she will be well insulated and protected from harm."

A good thing, so Jessie could be annoyed at her. "She's a traitor."

"I think she likes me," said Ewan.

"Well, don't feel too pleased about that. Maren likes everybody. She has quite literally never disliked someone until they proved that she ought to. And even then, she has a difficult time with it."

"But not you."

She looked at him out of the corner of her eye and denied the new tenderness surging through her.

Perhaps it was hormones.

That would be more comforting. More comforting at least than believing that proximity to him had done something permanent to her.

"I don't like anyone. As a matter of course."

"That's sage, Jessie. As people are in general useless."

"Where are we going?"

"Don't you want to be surprised?"

"I had thought that we had gotten to know each other at least a little bit."

"Be surprised, Jessie."

She felt stirred up as they boarded the beautiful private plane, which she still wasn't used to, and allowed herself to be served nonalcoholic drinks and cheeses.

She didn't know that she wanted to be surprised; it was yet another thing she couldn't envision. Couldn't label her trust.

She already thought she was wandering in a dark room, and she just wasn't accustomed to that feeling. She was used to having a reference door that she could open up in her mind to try and understand it. Even though sex with him had been *knowing*, she had a cursory understanding of the act and what it was.

She had been able to figure out exactly what should pass between them.

And even though the sensations of it had been something different, she had a guidebook, essentially.

And the guidebook felt important.

But there was no guidebook to this. She was afraid of what it might be, but even then, she had no way to look at it. No way to understand it. No way to examine it.

It was all just too much. A swelling feeling at the center of her chest, the tightening of her stomach, a restless sensation in her limbs.

This feeling that whatever was happening to her was too big for her body to sustain.

She was already carrying a baby so that just seemed unfair.

She was living life for another human. It seemed over-the-top.

But then, so had Ewan, from the first moment she had seen him.

She had never been the kind of person who could bring herself to believe in destiny. If destiny was real, then why had she been born to her father?

Divine Providence was difficult to latch on to when everything was just…hard. When you were left to the devices of a sociopathic madman; when your own brain was an enemy because it could be used as a weapon, either against her or… She had used it as such against other people. Even though she thought they deserved it.

But right now she wondered. Because when she went back to that moment she had first seen him…

It was so hard to say because there was no room for magical thinking in her world. Her brain trapped every detail, so remembering him had not seemed significant.

But it wasn't the remembering; it was that he had been there. In her path all the time, but she had difficulty sorting that out. Was it fate, or was she a mastermind? She had finagled her way into the game, but only through Maren's speaking to the right man.

Maybe this was the problem. She gave herself entirely too much credit. Because she gave herself so much credit, it was easy for her to dismiss anything slightly miraculous in the world.

She always figured it was because of her own machinations.

But maybe it wasn't.

She stuffed a slice of cheddar cheese into her mouth. Because at least that grounded her to the moment.

"Are you all right?" he asked, lounging back in the comfortable seat.

"Not especially. I would like to know where we're going."

"But don't you think it will be exciting to be caught unawares?"

"No. Because I'm a woman. Who has had to navigate the rather unfriendly streets of the world, and I can tell you, nothing good happens when you are caught unawares."

"This will be good."

"Do you intend to seduce me again?"

She tried to sound cool. But she rather hoped that he would.

"No. I intend to be true to my word. You wanted this to be a marriage in name only, and you will have your way."

What if, she said only to herself, *I have changed my mind?*

She didn't want to say it to him because she felt tender. Wounded.

She would have; only a week ago, she would have.

But since she'd had a chance to turn over everything that had passed between them in Paris, she didn't want to.

Because he was the *Starry Night*.

And she realized suddenly that when they'd made love when they'd been strangers, it had been like looking at a printed copy of that painting.

But this, knowing him, knowing the ways he had been hurt, knowing the ways his father had devastated him...

Confiding in him, being near him, sitting with the reality that she was carrying his baby. That they had made a child together...

These were the details of an original work of art. A masterpiece.

And she was overawed with them, and it made it impossible for her to keep her normally flippant facade up.

"Be surprised," he reiterated.

She napped, and when they landed hours later, the jewel-bright water was rushing up to greet them.

"Where are we?" she asked.

"An island in the Caribbean. Private, naturally. Easy to have supplies brought in daily, but we will be isolated. Not a soul in sight the entire time."

"That seems excessive."

"I thought we'd been through this already. I am excessive. In all things."

Except as she looked at him, she could see how much of that was a facade.

He had cultivated a persona of excess, but it was not who he was.

He was not the libertine that he pretended to be. Not that he hadn't engaged in the business pursuits, but she did not think he did so because he lacked self-control, or because hedonism was a siren's call he couldn't stay clear of. No, she had the feeling that it was all to do with his vengeance. And it irritated her that he was playing a part even with her, and yet… She shouldn't be surprised. She didn't think he had planned to let her guard down when he had told her about his mother. It had been circumstantial.

She intended to think about that more, but as soon as the plane door opened, a rush of fragrant floral air greeted her, and she could only step outside, her mouth dropped in awe.

"This will be our home for the month," he said.

"The month… And Maren will be safe the entire time?"

"Yes. Believe me. She has been moved somewhere equally luxurious, and just as private. Plus, she has an entire security detail surrounding her."

"Okay," she said cautiously.

Well, at least she would be able to rest. Yes, there were some difficulties emotionally. But she would be safe here from her father, and it was glorious.

A car whisked them along winding oceanside

roads, and she couldn't tear her gaze away from the water.

Crystal clear and an extraordinary shade of aqua all at once.

The white sands were so bright that she had to put on sunglasses to keep her eyes from burning.

They began a winding road that went away from the water, and up the mountain at the center of the island. And at first, she didn't see where they would be staying, but then suddenly, she saw it. Buried in the trees, a part of the landscape itself.

The house was on multiple levels, with bridges connecting different quadrants. It was made of honey-colored wood, with large windows that were highly reflective, and made it appear as if it was just more greenery, rather than a massive home.

"It's like a treehouse," she whispered.

She sounded more like Maren right then. Like she'd found something fresh and sweet inside herself.

She looked at him. He made her feel that way. It had scared her at first.

She liked it now.

She liked him.

"It is quite something," he said.

"Whose is it?"

"It's mine. One of the many properties I own."

"That's right. You have clubs. Sex clubs."

Her lips tingled when she said the words.

"I don't know that I would go so far as to call them that. But they are designed for people pursuing decadent pleasure, that is certain. The sex usually happens away from the club, though."

"Usually?"

"There are private rooms. And sometimes gatherings in there get…intimate."

"I see. And do you participate in such things?"

He shook his head. "No. To be honest with you, group sex has never appealed."

"That surprises me. You're an exhibitionist."

"No. I'm not an exhibitionist. I was making a show of certain things to build a facade. But I am not at my core someone who likes to expose every part of himself."

"I see."

It was all she could think to say. Because it made her think of that night in Paris, and what he'd said to her about his mother. And it made her realize that he was a man who kept many things tightly locked away.

It was true that she had a treasure trove of different personalities that she put off and on like the wigs that she had often worn during her gambling days.

But the Ewan that the world knew was a fully constructed personality that didn't exist.

She felt that she had seen under the persona

even that first night she'd been with him, but she wondered if he would ever admit that.

If he would ever acknowledge that she had truly met the man he was beneath it all.

She had her doubts.

He parked the car at the front of the house, and they got out. She looked around at the gardens, the paths that wound around the different quarters and quadrants of the building.

There were bridges above that stretched across rocky chasms and connected to different suites of rooms, and a staircase that went down below them, to a platform that seemed to extend well beyond the face of the mountain, likely offering glorious views.

"This place…"

"It is where I come to be alone."

And he had brought her.

"Well, it's beautiful."

When they walked up the path, the inside was glorious. Natural rock and slate tile, cement walls with cracks that had tropical vines growing through them, bright pink blooms adding color to the room.

Everything inside was both luxurious and natural all at once. And it was another thing she knew she would never forget. But for a moment she had forgotten that she was different. For a moment she had just been there, taking it all in.

Enjoying. As she had done that day in the art gallery. This was like art. This place.

"You will find that everything you need is already in your room."

"Thank you."

"It's up the stairs, and across the first bridge."

He didn't follow her, and she made her way up wood stairs that seemed to float and then down a long corridor that led to an enclosed glass walkway that stretched over the canopy of trees, and connected to another mountain ledge with a glorious suite that was all glass, offering an unobstructed view to the nature around it. The bed was white with white curtains surrounding it, and there was a giant deep tub. It was also beautiful. The most glorious honeymoon suite anyone could've ever thought of.

She smiled. And then she stretched across the bed and began to weep.

CHAPTER FOURTEEN

HE THOUGHT THAT he may have made a mistake leaving Jessie alone, and yet he found he needed the separation.

She was so devastatingly beautiful. And as his bride, she had been beautiful beyond belief.

He wanted her. He had never imagined taking a wife. Just as he had never imagined having a child.

But the sight of her in her white dress, her baby bump not concealed at all by the flowing fabric, had done something to him. And he could not afford to be in such a state.

He was doing this for the safety of her and the child.

By the time they returned from the island he anticipated that her father would be in prison.

He would be sure of it.

His investigators were working round the clock to find exactly what was needed to put the other man in prison for the rest of his life.

He would keep his family safe. He would…

They are not your family.
The only family you ever had died.
You are nothing but tragedy and poisoned blood.

And so he would leave Jessie to her isolation.

No matter how hurt she looked.

Because he was protecting her.

Whether she understood that or not.

She crept out into the main part of the house late that night.

She was starving.

It was true; her room contained everything she could possibly want.

There was a computer, and there were books. There were soft, silken pajamas, and she had put them on, then climbed into bed and read for several hours.

It was strange, to be so well taken care of. She had been grappling with that feeling ever since she had won the estate. Ever since she'd had enough. And hadn't had to work to keep herself comfortable.

But this was different still. A level of luxury she had yet to enjoy.

But now she was starving.

She walked back across the bridge, down the stairs, into the main part of the house.

The kitchen was a couple of levels higher than the living area, and she went inside and admired the beauty of it. More plants everywhere, and concrete countertops gave it a natural cave-like feeling.

But mostly, she was headed right for the overlarge fridge. She opened it up and saw platters of prepared foods, and took one out eagerly, uncovering it and taking some fruit off of the board while she continued to look inside.

"I see that you found what you require."

She turned around and saw him standing there. He was wearing a pair of sweatpants, low on his hips, and no shirt. There was sweat beaded there on his muscles and she thought he might've been working out.

Hunger was what kept her up. And missing him. She wondered what kept him up.

"I skipped dinner. And I don't skip meals. Not right now. Not ever."

"When you were with your father did he make sure you had plenty to eat?"

She shrugged. "I suppose so."

Her gaze kept going back to his chest as if it was a magnet. And she tried to cast her mind back to living at her father's compound. That was not a sexy thought. Not in the least.

"You don't sound definitive."

"It wasn't about us. It was, at best, about my father and his wants and needs. He had a private chef that provided him with whatever he wanted. His favorites."

She rooted around the fridge, looking for something specific; she just wasn't sure what. She only knew she would know when she saw it. "I remember when Maren and I escaped and we had our first win. We went and bought a whole bunch of things from the grocery store, and tasted them all. And we went out to a restaurant and we ordered everything. Trying to figure out what our favorite foods are."

"And what did you decide?"

"I love breakfast sandwiches. Eggs and bacon and cheese. On a croissant. Maren prefers cereal. I love pasta of all kinds. Though specifically ravioli. I think it's delicious. I love Caesar salad."

"I think you might find one of those in there. And some pasta."

She did and managed to make herself a large bowl of salad, and then reheated some pasta with lemon and vinegar and sat down at the concrete countertop, eating quickly, and under his far too careful gaze.

"What about you?" she asked around a mouthful of lettuce. "What are your favorite foods?"

"I don't know."

"What?"

"I don't know. I have been fed a steady diet of the best and richest foods that the world's top chefs have to offer. I've never really thought about what was better or worse."

Because he was never him. He was the playboy. And it wasn't actually about pleasing himself, but about crafting a personality aimed at his father.

She'd been grappling with similar. She'd cut her feelings off so she could avoid pain, and sorrow and disturbing memories, but he replaced all that with enough good she didn't need it.

Not anymore.

She looked at him, at his beautiful face, and she put her hand on her rounded stomach.

It was a revelation.

The bad was still there. All her memories. Especially the one that haunted her, of the way her father had hurt that child, had used her to gain access to that child.

For the first time she was able to feel...like it was finished. The child had gotten away; Jessie had helped her. Her memory had kept the bad part of it alive, so vivid it was like she'd never really gotten out.

But she had. And somehow standing there with her future in front of her, with the possibility of good things feeling bigger than what had gone on before it, she could find the good that much easier.

And there was so much good.

"Well, we can't have that. You need to figure out what your favorite food is."

"Why?"

"Because everyone should know that. Food

is one of the most glorious indulgences that we have been given as humans. Taste is purely for pleasure."

"That is actually not true. Taste also tells us if something is poison."

She sniffed. "I like my version of that better."

"It doesn't make it true."

His logic was both sound and infuriating.

"Well, be that as it may. Taste buds are one of the few frivolous parts of our bodies."

"Not the *only*, though. I believe there is one part of a woman's body that exists only for pleasure."

His eyes met hers and she felt a fizz of desire skate down her spine. Her internal muscles clenched tight, and she wanted to cross the distance between them and slap him on the shoulder.

Because it was mean to bring that up. Especially when he was refusing to seduce her.

You're seduced. Utterly, entirely and permanently. You could just seduce him.

She could. But she was enjoying the conversation. And the problem with them was she already knew the sex was good. But they hadn't had conversations like this.

"That is true. But that part of your body does not tell you if something is poison. Something very bad can feel very good."

"I suppose that is also true."

"But in the interest of pleasurable pursuits, I

do think that we need to figure out what your favorite food is."

"Shall I place an order to the mainland?"

"Yes. And we shall have a tasting. That's what I want to do. For our honeymoon. But it can't all be good foods. You have to get packaged foods. Processed foods. From America. Because they are the best ones."

"You say that with a great deal of authority."

"I *know* so. We did another grocery trip our first time back to America. We grew up there, you see, but of course, then moved to England."

"Yes. I did realize that."

"So we shall place an order."

"I'll leave that to you, Jessie, since you're the one with so many opinions."

"You're about to get a few more of your own."

CHAPTER FIFTEEN

HE DIDN'T KNOW quite why he had allowed his wife to take the wheel on this. Perhaps because it didn't matter. Perhaps because it made her happy, and that made him want to... He wasn't exactly sure. Make her smile, perhaps, because she had been quite unhappy with him right after the wedding.

And this had seemingly made her happy, and that made him... It was something.

When he came downstairs after spending a few hours going over his accounts, two days after they had first arrived at the house, he found Jessie sitting with a pile of food packages around her, and a wide grin on her face. "I'm setting up a tasting."

"Jessie, this is maniacal." He looked around and saw boxes of unnaturally colored toaster pastries, and brightly colored cereals and that was just the breakfast section.

"They were able to fly in hamburgers from a couple of restaurant chains. They're in these little thermal containers to keep them warm. Is it not delightful?"

"It's insane."

"Come be insane with me, then. We are going to figure out what your actual favorite food is."

He'd never thought about it because he didn't care. He was powered by the desire for revenge. The need to destroy his father. The need to play the part that he was required to in order to accomplish what he wanted to.

Build his own empire. Disgrace that family name. Then he had done so. Along the way, there had been pleasures, but none of it had been specific. The food had been good. The sex was satisfying.

Being with Jessie was specific. And now she was asking him to find that with food.

It was a strange thing, and yet he found he couldn't deny her.

"All right," he said, sitting down on the low sofa across from all the food. "Bring me something to eat."

She picked up a box of toaster pastries and laughed happily while she opened it. "These are my favorite. They're wild berry."

"Is a wild berry neon blue and purple?"

"These magical mystical wild berries that are fashioned in a lab are. And they're delicious. All we have to do is put them in the toaster." She took the little silver package and shook it in front of him. "Come on."

"This is very strange, and so are you," he said.

"You say that like it's something that should bother me. But you know that it doesn't. I'm perfectly happy being strange. I never had a hope of being normal."

Neither of them had, he supposed. The toaster pastry heated quickly, and he could honestly say he wasn't a fan. She took it from him and finished what he didn't. "Too sweet, you say?" she asked.

"Definitively."

"We can probably skip the sugary cereal, then. But I find that highly suspicious."

"What do you find suspicious?"

"That anything could be too sweet."

From there they went on to hamburgers and French fries; he did have a definitive favorite there. What had to be the cheapest one, that had an association with arches, he believed.

"I don't know why it's good," he said, taking another bite.

"It shouldn't be," she said. "Objectively speaking. And yet, it is. Absolutely delicious."

He couldn't disagree. He'd had some of the best gourmet food in the world, and yet, he could see this being something he wanted again and again.

Jessie demanded that he rank and score everything, and by the time they were finished, it was dark outside, and he felt vaguely ill.

But Jessie looked cheerful, and she was still snacking on chips.

"So we have your favorites. A favorite fast food, and you have decided that your favorite overall food is…"

"Steak."

"That is incredibly masculine of you."

She had scooted closer to him during their tastings, and he found that looking at her too closely was like staring at a sunrise full on.

And then she drew closer to him, and he knew what she intended to do. And he found himself unable to turn away from her.

She pressed her mouth to his, and it was like the world had stopped.

"You're the only man I've ever kissed," she whispered against his lips.

"Perhaps we should bring an array of men to the island."

Even as a joke, he didn't care for it. Even as something that would never actually come to pass, he hated it.

"It's funny," she said. "I know that I don't need to. Because when I was a girl, and I saw other foods on TV shows, foods that were not my father's favorites, I wanted them. And as soon as I had the opportunity I went out and I made sure I got them. Because you know how I am. I never forget. And because I never forget I remembered each and every food that I wished I could try that

I'd been denied. I hold on to things. And that gives me a certain certainty about my cravings, I suppose. But I could've had any man I wished. And yes, Maren and I had rules. But you know me. I'm happy to violate Maren's rules if it suits me."

"Yes," he said, his voice rough.

"I don't need to kiss a whole line of men to know that kissing you is my favorite thing."

"This should not go further," he said, his voice rough. But he didn't know where that came from. The need to make her keep her distance.

"It doesn't have to. I am content to simply kiss you. Because we didn't do that the first time. We raced right ahead." She pressed her mouth to his again, and it was so soft and sweet. He had never kissed simply for the pleasure of it, but with her, he found himself settling right into it. He put his hand on her cheek and parted his lips, letting her tangle her tongue with his. Letting himself get caught up in the moment. He found himself cupping her face, smoothing his thumbs along her jaw as he kissed her deeper and deeper.

She moaned, and it took all the self-control he had not to push her flat on her back, amongst all the food wrappers, and have her then and there.

But she had said they would only kiss. And it was foolish to do anything else.

Because his control had been severely compromised the last time he had been with her.

What control? Already she's pregnant with your baby.

He pulled away from her, and the soft smile on her face nearly undid him. Yes. He had indulged himself all these years. With rich food and with more lovers than he could count. And yet, none of it had ever really mattered. And it was because of how big the moment felt that he pulled back now.

"I have a new favorite thing to add to my list."

His voice was so rough it was barely recognizable even to himself. And he waited, waited to see if she would move back and kiss him again, because if she did, then he would be overtaken. If she did, he would not be able to resist her.

But instead, she sat back, with a sweet smile on her face.

"So do I."

CHAPTER SIXTEEN

THEY DIDN'T MAKE LOVE. For two weeks they were on the island, and they didn't make love.

They talked. About food now, since he knew what his favorites were, and about his friends at school.

It was difficult to dig deep enough to get to a personal part of Ewan. Because it was clear to Jessie that he had done everything he could to minimize that part of himself.

It was all related to the fact he hadn't even known his own favorite foods. The degree to which he had given himself over to his desire to hurt his father had shaped everything he was.

It was frightening, sometimes.

He seemed like a warm, carefree playboy, and he was anything but.

It scared her sometimes, wondering how deep that core of destruction went within him. And if there was anything of a man left.

But that night when he had kissed her, just

kissed her, she had found something helpful to hold on to.

You're just as broken as he is.

Sometimes the voice whispered to her. Like now, when she was walking through the outdoor bridge system up inside the trees, enjoying the weather and the view through the fronds of the ocean below.

Sometimes that voice whispered to her that she wasn't different. That this time away hadn't transformed her.

She remembered what Maren had said.

That they were nothing more than women experiencing con artistry.

She had never needed that sort of buffer between herself and the decision she'd made.

She had seen herself as a con artist.

But what was she now? She was a woman about to have a baby.

She was…

She was falling in love with him.

They'd gone about everything all backward. Inside out. Except perhaps they hadn't. Because the moment that she'd met him something had taken hold of her that she had not been able to get rid of since.

The moment she had first laid eyes on him.

He had made her feel things she'd never felt before, and she'd been driven by them.

If they'd struck up a conversation first, they both would have run in the other direction.

They had both constructed their entire lives in such a way that it had made them unable to get to know people. He had been surrounded by revelers, by parties for all these years, and yet he didn't even know himself. And Jessie knew only Maren and protected her actual identity above all else.

It was almost necessary, then, that they'd made love first. Which had bonded them together by way of the baby.

She had been thinking more and more about the baby, too. As not just a baby, but a baby that would grow into a child.

A child who would need a mother.

She had never known what a real mother was supposed to do, what a real mother was supposed to be. She had images, saved in her files of TV and book moms, and the flashes of brilliance that her own had brought to her life before she had left forever.

But she didn't want to be a mother constructed simply of images.

Of knowledge.

She was learning that she needed to begin to build things from her heart.

And there was no certainty there.

She was so used to certainty.

To the absolutes of her mind, and life was more than absolutes. It was these messy uncertain spaces, where she had to do battle with her own doubts. Where she had to try to find a picture of something that she had never seen before and figure out how to walk toward that.

An image of herself holding her baby. An image of herself hugging a small child before that child went to school.

Of loving that child when they were messy, crying and inconvenient.

Of giving that child all the things she had never had.

Love, she realized, filled the blank spaces. It was love that allowed you to feel what you could never know.

Love was the most important thing, and it wasn't as simple as something you kept in a file in your mind.

She felt changed out here. With so many fewer things to see you, and know and learn.

Left behind with only her feelings.

With the silence of the trees and the sounds of the waves.

With the beat of her heart, and the need in her soul to find more than what she had been given up until this point.

She didn't know what she was doing. But she would use love to fill in the spaces.

She was very afraid that she was beginning to love him.

Very, very afraid.

Because she wasn't sure what more he had inside. Because she wasn't sure if there was more to him. She wanted there to be. There were moments when she was almost certain.

You know what you have to do.

She did. But it was frightening.

But they had done all this backward. Sex first, a baby and now they had gotten to know each other.

But there was still more in him. She was certain of it. There was still a part of himself that he held back.

And she realized that they were at the point now. The point where she ought to seduce him.

Because it meant something different now.

Because they had changed.

She had cut her feelings off to protect herself from the horror of their lives. From the pain she'd caused due to her father's machinations. So much so that she had, for a time, forgotten what feeling was. So much so that she had denied it to the point that she was afraid she didn't have it.

She had stopped protecting herself in some ways, but she was still clinging on to pieces of that protection.

She had to stop. Because that was the key to change. To her actually becoming new. To her actually being the mother she needed to be. The sister she wanted to be.

The woman she had always wished she could be.

And that meant taking a chance.

The risk. But this was different from gambling. When you gambled, the prize wasn't specific. Not generally. It was just a pot of whatever the fools decided to gamble. And this was only her heart.

That was all. And it had to be him, or it would be nothing and no one.

That isn't true.

Even if he can't do this, you'll have your child. Even if he can't do this, you'll have Maren.

All the ways that you've changed.

It was true. She would.

It fortified her. It made her feel strong.

She grasped the railing on the bridge and looked out at the view, then tilted her head back. And took in a deep breath.

She didn't connect the moment to memory; she didn't go in and open up her files. She simply was. She simply felt.

And she smiled.

Because she could do that now. And somehow she knew that it would be okay. That it had to be.

A sliver of fear wound its way through her. Because perhaps, for a while, it would feel like it wasn't okay.

Perhaps for a while, she would be broken.

And she would have to figure out how to put herself together again.

But she was strong.

She knew that she was.

She was Jessie Hargreave. And she wasn't the con woman her father had made her.

She was the woman she had decided to make herself.

Looking at Jessie had become almost a physical pain. Ewan had never experienced such a thing before. He had never desired a woman and denied himself that woman. He had never desired anything and denied it. Because he had never allowed anything to become bigger than his pursuit of revenge.

And yet, it was gone. That revenge. The thing that had made him who he was. And he had experienced that moment of emptiness. Then he transferred it. To Jessie's father. He was fine when he was being driven by a desire to destroy.

Hands that wanted nothing more than destruction could never touch Jessie.

And so he didn't.

Apart from that kiss they had shared two weeks ago.

But it was killing him. Killing him to deny himself.

Because denial was associated with being controlled.

And somewhere in the middle of all this it had ceased to be about his control over himself and had begun to feel like the torture he had experienced as a child.

This need to make himself into something acceptable. Something different.

He walked across the bridge from the room he was using as his office, and into his bedroom, and stopped. Because Jessie was standing there in the middle of the room. Naked.

Her brown hair was loose around her shoulders, long enough just to brush the tops of her breasts, not long enough to conceal the tightened, dusky buds there.

Her belly was rounded from her pregnancy, and it aroused him deeply. Filled him with a sense of triumph to see her changed by him.

Her hips were generous and lovely; the dark triangle at the apex of her thighs made his mouth water.

And there was no thought to be given to control. Not now. Not in this moment.

"I like talking," she said. "Don't get me wrong. But I did think that perhaps we were missing something that this honeymoon needed badly."

She took a step toward him, and that was all he needed.

He released his hold on everything. On his control, on everything that was tethering them to the earth, and moved to her, wrapping his arm around her waist and drawing her flush against his body.

"I want you," he said, the words guttural.

"I want you," she said. "But I want all of you. All the things that you are. All the things that you hide. I made myself my mind. Only my mind, and it was only when I made love with you that I was able to turn it off for the first time in my life. That night we were together, all I did was feel. I was not crowded with thoughts. And ever since then, even if it has taken work, I have been able to find my way back to that place, because now I know what it is. You gave me a gift. You allowed me to unlock a door inside myself and walk into a room that I did not know was there.

"It is all me. But it is me that I kept hidden. The part of myself that I kept most protected. And I learned something. That it is not protection. It is prison. I kept that part of myself imprisoned. What do you keep locked away?"

She was searching him, her gaze far too keen, far too sharp. And he wanted to turn away from her. He wanted to tell her there was nothing. Nothing.

Because he had not locked a part of himself away; he had hollowed himself out. Bled himself dry the way that his mother had done.

Because there had been no choice for him that day. No other way for him to survive.

And as he looked at her, suddenly that glory he'd felt a moment before over seeing her round with his baby was overshadowed by fear.

Fear.

That was what he kept locked away.

Because as long as he was vengeance, then

he was out there taking control of the world and making things right. Balancing the scales.

But the truth that it hid, the thing that he denied the most, was that he would never be able to stop injustice.

He would only be able to fight it afterward, again and again.

But there were some things in this world that you could not stop. Some things that you could not ever have dominion over, and that was the thing that frightened him most.

It was the thing that made him feel like a small boy who walked out in the cold, starving and freezing.

And the worst thing was it was his father who held the key to all of that; it was…some power that simply laughed at the misfortune and destruction of humanity.

For he was angry at his father for a great many things; his father had been forever the demon in his life, but his father had not killed his mother, and he had not killed his brother.

It had been a force that he could not seek vengeance on. A force that he could not control.

And he would never be able to protect Jessie, either. He would never be able to protect the child.

He pushed those thoughts away, and growled, kissing her with all that he was.

He would not speak anymore.

He knew how to deny all of this. He knew how to keep it hidden.

How to keep it secret.

He knew.

So he opened up the part of himself that embraced nothing but feeling, sensation, and he consumed her.

He moved his hands over her smooth, soft curves, kissed her neck and down to the plump swells of her breasts.

He took one nipple deep in his mouth and sucked hard until she cried out.

"You're more sensitive now," he growled, his mouth against her flesh.

"Ewan."

The way she said his name, broken and pleading, ignited a fire inside him.

And he decided to let it burn him.

Because at least that was all-consuming enough to block out everything else.

He kissed his way down her body, that rounded swell of her stomach, and he refused to let himself think.

He buried his head between her thighs, licking that sweet center of her.

He had missed her. He had missed this.

"My very favorite delicacy," he growled.

The broken cry that was elicited from her lovely mouth told him everything he needed to know.

She was as lost to this as he was.

They didn't need to bring their conversations to this.

They didn't need to bring the changes that had happened between them these past weeks. This could be sex. Simply.

As it had been the first time.

It was never just sex. It was never simple.

He remembered. The first time he'd seen her.

In the way he'd known was awake even then.

That moment in the casino, and had never gone away from him. Not one detail lessened by time.

As if it was one of Jessie's memories, and she had planted it in his own mind.

He pushed back against that, licked her deeper until she was screaming, until she was trembling.

Until he tasted her climax over and over.

He tried to picture other women. Tried to make this familiar, but all he could see was her.

All the times he had seen her.

As if the path to this moment was inevitable. As if it was fate.

He refused to believe in something so cruel as fate.

He refused.

How could it take his mother from him, and give him his father? How could it give him Jessie when he was too twisted and destroyed to care for her in the way that she deserved?

No. He could not believe it was fate.

He could not.

He stood up, lifting her off the floor and wrapping her legs around his waist as he carried her to the bed. He consumed her. Took her mouth with his and claimed her utterly and thoroughly. Did everything he could to block out the thoughts that crowded his mind.

But nothing could block out the feelings that bled into his chest.

He felt like he was dying. Like something inside him was shattering.

When he brought her up over his body and thrust deep inside her, looked up at the view of her, over him, his hardness buried deep within her, he felt undone.

As if he would never be able to separate from her again. As if he would never be whole again if he could not be inside her like this for all time.

The picture that she made was so erotic he could barely breathe.

Her rounded stomach, her glorious breasts. The expression of pure ecstasy on her face.

She was glorious, and at that moment, she was perhaps everything.

And so he lost himself, in the rhythm that she created as she began to flex her hips. As her internal muscles rippled around him, she began to climb closer and closer to another climax, and he found himself perilously close to the edge of the same.

He had made a mistake. Because this wasn't

the same. He had thought that if he was in her again, it would all be familiar. Because not only had he been with countless women, he had her before as well.

He had thought it would bring them back to familiar territory, but this wasn't.

It was new. It was something bright and wholly different than anything he'd ever had before.

He'd had sex.

This was making love.

This was what happened when your soul saw someone, and they saw you, and then your bodies became one.

This was something he had never believed in. More than that, it was something he had never wanted.

Because this…

This was the precipice of a man's sanity.

This was him, unmasked.

This was him, without any of the artifice, any of the control.

This was where a loss would make him jump off to the jagged rocks below, and damn the consequences.

This could make a man destroy everything around him, and he was powerless to fight against it.

Powerless to do anything but surrender.

To her, to this.

To the need that pounded through him.

It was the one thing he had vowed never to do. The one thing he had never done. At the hands of his father, under the fist of his grief, he had never surrendered.

And yet, in her arms, buried in her body, he could do nothing but.

He shouted his release as she gave a hoarse cry and found her own, and he was lost. Spiraling into the darkness. But there was light there. And he did not want it. There was light there, but it frightened him more than anything else ever had.

And then she whispered. Into that light.

"I love you."

And just after that, his phone rang.

CHAPTER SEVENTEEN

SHE WAS STILL SPENT in the aftermath of what had passed between them, her body vibrating with the pleasure that she'd found in his arms, and he was moving to the nightstand, grabbing his phone. "Yes?"

She listened intently, worry for her sister filling her chest.

"I see. Thank you." He hung up the phone. "Your father is dead."

She did not know what she had expected to feel under the weight of such an announcement.

But the burst of joy that went through her was not expected. Still, she supposed it was fair.

He had threatened her baby, and he was gone.

He was gone. All the power that he'd had all this time over her life, over her choices, over her safety, and he was gone.

"What happened?"

"He decided to have a gunfight with the police rather than going quietly. It is better this way, Jessie. Even from prison, he could have…"

"I know," she said. "I do. I… I know that it's for the best. I'm not sad."

"Good," he said. "It's a good thing, too, that I am confident now that I'm not without feeling because I might've thought so now. It's cold-blooded to be happy that your father is dead, I suppose.

"But it's for our baby. I am happy for our child that he won't be there to cast a shadow over their life."

"No. He is gone."

And she realized then they didn't need to stay married. Because she was safe. Maren was safe.

There were choices now.

Choices she'd never had before.

This was real freedom.

"I'm free," she said.

"You are," he agreed.

And she looked at Ewan, and she knew that his father's death had not brought that same freedom.

She wished that she could fix it. That she could break open the thing inside him that still held them in chains, but she didn't know what it was, and she didn't know how.

She felt helpless then. Helpless to do anything but hold on to him. "I love you," she said. "I want to say it now, now that I have all the choices in the world. All the freedom in the world. Nothing is hanging over me, and nothing holding me back. I love you."

"Jessie…"

"Why don't you feel the same? Why did your father dying not make you feel this? Because I no longer live underneath his shadow, and neither do you."

"It isn't that simple."

"Why not? Why does he get to decide who you are, what you are? He was cruel, unimaginably so. He left a little boy to wallow in his grief, and he caused him more pain."

"I thought that when my father died, I thought that when I got my revenge on him, everything would be right. But it wasn't. I was left with nothing more than emptiness, and do you know why?"

"Why?"

"Because my mother is still dead. He did not kill her. My brother is still dead, and he did not kill him. It was…the hand of fate. I don't know. But they are dead, and there is nothing in this whole world that I could do to fix it. Revenge did not fix it. Nothing can. The world is the same as it ever was for me."

She shook her head. "No. It isn't. Don't say that. Yes, tragic things happen. They do, and we can't control those things, but they don't get to decide…"

"They do. Jessie, I could not bear watching you bleed out. I could not lose you. I cannot…"

"Isn't that love?"

"If it is then I want nothing to do with it."

"You can't stop it from happening if it's going

to happen," she said. "You can't will it away. You cannot be vengeful enough to blot out what will be, or to take away your own feelings, and why should you? I did that. For so many years. I ignored my own feelings. I denied them."

"I don't want you away from me. I could not stand it. Not now. But I'd... I cannot be what you are asking. I can never soften myself. I can never..."

"Then I won't stay with you."

It cut her open to say it. It made her want to die. Then and there. Just lie down on the floor and stop breathing altogether because it seemed easier than bearing such a loss.

"I love you, Ewan. I have never let myself love. Not anyone other than my sister. I never let myself be wanted. I never let myself feel. But I do now. I do now. And I just want more than anything in the world for you to love me back. I want us to win. I don't want the dark things to win. I don't want the terrible things to win. And believe me, I know, because I remember. There are endless stories where the darkness wins and the hero dies. But there are also stories where they live. We have to choose it. We have to choose to live. All the way. With everything we are. We have to choose to do it with the fullness of ourselves because no one will choose it for us. The world is tragic. But I am choosing to trust in what I cannot see. And what I know in my heart to be true.

There is no file in my brain that tells me that everything will be fine. That it will be fine. But I believe it in my soul."

"I cannot."

"Let me believe it for the both of us. If I can do that, if I can have just a small bit of hope that someday... That someday you can, then I don't need to walk away from you."

"I can't," he said.

And something inside her broke away. Something she knew that she would never get back. "You know where I am."

"Jessie..."

"I just can't, Ewan. Not after everything. I want to be loved. The way that I love. Because you are my favorite thing. And I don't need to taste an array of pleasures in this world to know that. To know that you are what I want. To know that you are what I need, too. You helped me find all these things out about myself. And I tried to do the same for you. I can't be less to you than you are to me."

He said nothing. He simply stood there, naked and ragged, his body so beautiful it made her want to weep, his eyes so full of pain that she did.

"I'm going to call the private plane. I'm going to go home."

She turned and walked away from him, walked across the bridge, and made her way down to the main part of the house before her knees gave out.

Before she began to weep. Even as she took out her phone and put in the order for the private jet.

She had to do this. Because she had to trust.

In the evidence of things she could not see. In the gaps that her mind could not know.

In love.

Because it was the newest and greatest thing she had learned. And hope, because it was what it was saying to her soul even now.

Because she had been a woman without those things. She had been hard and isolated and lonely.

She didn't know everything, it turned out. But she knew this.

But in the end, love was worth taking a stand for.

And she had to hope that it was bigger than vengeance could ever be.

She was gone. And he felt gutted. Hollowed out.

It was not the first time he'd felt this way. It was a grief that transcended breath.

He should let her walk away. He should let her go and find happiness. With someone else, somewhere else.

What could he possibly give to her? What could he possibly give to a child?

Nothing.

As long as your hands are bound by fear.

It was the truth, and he knew it; he simply didn't know where it came from.

What untried part of his soul had this level of wisdom?

He had made himself nothing.

And when his father died that had become apparent, because he had lost his purpose and his meaning.

Now that her father was dead, he felt the same. Except… She was still here.

She was still here, and the promise of his child yet existed.

When his father died, his mother had still been gone. His brother had still been dead.

And he had felt helpless in the face of that reality. Of that grief.

Jessie was still here. And that meant that at this moment he was choosing fear over her. Over his child.

And that made him rage.

At himself. At everything he was.

He had rejected her.

And he was nothing now, nothing more than that boy who'd walked away.

Dammit all, his father still held the keys.

He had never escaped. The vengeance had never been his.

He had spent all these years drinking poison and waiting for it to kill his father. His father had died of old age. His father had died after a long, bitter life.

Ewan had been allowing his father to kill him. All these years.

What he could be; what he could have.

Any hopes, any dreams, any love.

Jessie. He wanted Jessie.

He wanted to feel no fear so that he could have her.

You won't. You always have the memory of your mother. You will always have the memory of your brother.

He sat there in that certainty. It was true.

He would always remember their deaths. He would always remember that tragedy. And the abuse that had followed.

He had to accept it. Something that happened. Something that was part of him.

And he had to find it in himself to choose to have more.

To be more than pain and suffering. To be more than his father had allowed him to be.

He had to stop letting that old man destroy him.

He had to stop letting tragedy define who he was.

Otherwise, his child would be marked by these things as well. Forever and ever.

He had to stop it.

He had fought to break the chain by stopping his bloodline. But he realized something now.

He had to break it even with his bloodline carrying on. And it was not something fate would handle for him.

He had to do it himself. He had to break those chains with his own hands.

And by God, he would.

Because Jessie loved him.

Despite all that she'd been through, she loved him.

Despite everything she knew and all the things she remembered, she loved him.

He did not remember everything. But he knew that when he drew his last breath he would remember seeing her for the first time. Remember watching her look at that painting. Remember her standing naked in his room ready to seduce him. He knew that those memories could become bigger than the ones that held all of his pain.

But only if you let them.

Only if you let this love be bigger than fear.

He stood up and turned the knob on his bedroom door. It was not locked.

Because he was not a prisoner. Not anymore. It was simply a matter of choosing to walk out of the cell.

And so he did.

For her.

For love.

CHAPTER EIGHTEEN

MAREN HAD PROVIDED food and fuzzy blankets upon Jessie's arrival. She had shouted invectives and made physical threats of violence while Jessie cried.

"I will kill him!" Maren announced. "With... pillows. I'll smother him."

It almost made Jessie laugh.

"No, Maren, you don't need to engage in soft murder on my behalf."

It was clear that she was unnerved by the fact that it was not Jessie who was being bloodthirsty.

But she simply didn't have it in her.

Not right now.

Mostly because she wasn't angry at him, as much as she would like to be.

She was just sad.

"Love really does sound terrible," said Maren.

"It is," said Jessie. "But wonderful all at once. I wouldn't trade it. I wouldn't go back. Because

I'm finally who I want to be because of all of this."

"I don't think I understand that."

Jessie laughed. "I don't think I do, either."

Maren had gone to a meeting about the acquisition of her new property, and Jessie was still lying on a chaise longue next to a window in the estate when she saw the sleek white plane begin its descent.

Her heart leaped.

"No," she whispered. "Don't do that. Don't hope."

No. Hope. Because you can. She stood up, and she found herself walking out the door, and then running.

Running up over the grassy hills that led to the landing strip.

And then she saw him. Just on the other side. Barefoot. And running toward her.

"At him," she whispered.

And as much as she could, she ran toward him.

And when she reached him, he pulled her into his embrace, and simply held her.

"I love you," he said, his whisper fierce and hard.

"I love you, too."

She couldn't wait to hear his explanation. All the things that had shifted and changed inside him. But she didn't need them to know that she loved him.

She didn't need them for this moment.

"I'm sorry that I was afraid."

"Life gave you a lot of reasons to be afraid."

"I could never believe in fate. I thought it seemed cruel. But right now it doesn't. I thought that I needed to destroy myself to destroy my father. But there are more ways to break a cycle than I believed. We can break it now. By being different. By choosing love. By choosing that over power. Over all else."

"Yes," she whispered.

"I love you, Jessie. More than I'm afraid of losing you. More than I'm afraid of pain. I love you more than all the pain and suffering and glory on this earth. And I always will."

"I love you, too."

Jessie Hargreave had been raised to believe that there were two kinds of people. The frightened and the frightening. She had believed the only way to beat that system was to be a con artist. Someone who wove her way through the margins of fear. But now she realized that none of that was true at all.

Because there was love.

And it changed people. It changed them from frightened creatures, it changed them from con artists, into something wholly beautiful, wholly wonderful. And entirely worthy.

And from their love they would grow enough

good, big, beautiful memories to make the darkness seem small.

She knew without a doubt, that what she would teach her child was that in the end, the greatest thing of all was love.

EPILOGUE

EWAN DIDN'T BREATHE the entire time Jessie was in labor. He had chosen love, but it didn't mean that his bad memories didn't still exist inside him.

Part of embracing the truth of himself had been grieving. His father had cut his grieving short, and then after that he'd cut off his own grief so he could embrace his chosen persona.

So now he felt sad sometimes when he thought of his mother. Anger when he thought of his father. A peculiar sense of missing something when he thought of the baby brother he'd never had a chance to know.

Above all else, when he looked at Jessie, he felt love.

So even though his emotions weren't all pleasant all the time, the love was always there.

But his daughter was born screaming and healthy. And Jessie was laughing and beaming within moments of their daughter being placed on her chest.

And that was when he realized that things could be okay.

That he could have something glorious and beautiful.

That he was truly able to be more.

Now he had a family. His wife, their little girl. Even Maren had become as a sister to him, and that had healed that broken part of himself that had lost a sibling.

His life was full now.

And he was himself. As he'd always been meant to be.

No masks. No games.

He leaned in and kissed his wife on the temple, and brushed his finger along his daughter's downy cheek. "I love you." He let out a long sigh. "I was willing to endure pain to love you. But I realize now even more... I want to be happy. Loving you. I'm ready for joy."

She looked up at him and smiled, and he knew right there was all the joy he would ever need. "So am I."

* * * * *

If The Billionaire's Accidental Legacy
blew you away, then you're sure to get lost in
the next installment of the
From Destitute to Diamonds duet,
The Christmas the Greek Claimed Her.
Coming soon!

And don't forget to dive into these other stories
by Millie Adams!

Crowning His Innocent Assistant
The Only King to Claim Her
His Secretly Pregnant Cinderella
The Billionaire's Baby Negotiation
A Vow to Set the Virgin Free

Available now!